NOBODY BUT US

NOBODY
BUT US

KRISTIN HALBROOK

An Imprint of HarperCollinsPublishers

HarperTeen is an imprint of HarperCollins Publishers.

Nobody But Us
www.epicreads.com

Library of Congress Cataloging-in-Publication Data
Halbrook, Kristin.
    Nobody but us / Kristin Halbrook. — 1st ed.
        p.   cm.
    Summary: Told in their separate voices, eighteen-year-
old Will, who has aged out of foster care, and fifteen-year-old
Zoe, whose father beats her, set out for Las Vegas together,
but their escape may prove more dangerous than what they
left behind.
    ISBN 978-0-06-212126-4
    [1. Runaways—Fiction. 2. Fugitives from justice—
Fiction. 3. Automobile travel—Fiction. 4. Love—Fiction.
5. Family problems—Fiction. 6. Foster home care—Fiction.
7. West (U.S.)—Fiction.]   I. Title.
PZ7.H12837Nob 2013   2012011526
[Fic]—dc23   CIP
                                                         AC

Typography by Torborg Davern
13 14 15 16 17   CG/RRDH   10 9 8 7 6 5 4 3 2 1
❖
First Edition

To Mom, who always thought I should,
And Dad, who always knew I could,
With love.

NOBODY BUT US

ZOE

HE COMES DOWN THE ROAD IN HIS CAMARO SLIDING
left to right on the freshly oiled gravel and skidding to a stop
in front of my house. He's driving so fast that I'm sure my
dad is going to rouse from his drunken stupor and catch me
before I can get out of the house.

"Geez, Will, you want to wake him up?" I hiss as he gets
out of the car and slams the door shut.

Will looks up to my window and crunches across the
gravel toward me, twirling the keys on his finger.

"Hell, he's more plastered than the house," he jokes with
a dopey grin.

I roll my eyes and push myself away from the window ledge.

The zipper on my duffel bag and the clasp on my makeup case are securely closed. The window screen gives me more trouble than usual, but I fiddle with it for a minute. Finally, it comes out of its guide and falls to the ground with a clatter that rends the still night.

"Yeah, I'm the noisy one," Will mutters.

"Shh!"

I toss the duffel down to him, followed by the case. He makes a quick run to his car and stashes the items on the backseat, then returns to his spot under the window.

"Ready?" I whisper. My heart races and my head swims as I take in the space between us. Relax, Zoe, it's the same drop you've done before.

"Drop, baby," Will says, holding his hands out to me.

I take a slow breath. Climb into the window frame. He waits there, below me, that same eager look in his eyes he always has. Maybe they're brighter this time. Or maybe it's me, seeing something brighter to come.

"Come on, Zoe. I'll never drop you."

"I know."

I close my eyes. The swirling in my vision stops, but my stomach buckles. I sway. Then I push off. The one-second fall feels like an eternity of stomach-in-my-throat weight-lessness, but Will catches me. I throw my arms around him and seek his mouth, kissing him.

"I have to get my chimes."

"I already told you, they're too big to hang from the mirror."

"I know. But I'm not leaving them here for him."

Will sets me on my feet, and I dash up the three steps to the front porch. The chimes are in the corner. They were my mom's and now they're mine. I drag a chair over and push it against the railing, climb up, and balance precariously on the edge of the chair. The chimes tinkle a greeting at me as I reach for them, the dolphins brushing up against the steel rods in the center.

I lift the chimes off their hook with one hand and coddle the metal pieces with the other. They make too much noise, but I have them. I step down and peer into the living room window. My dad, who had fallen asleep in his recliner, like he does most nights of the week, stinking of whiskey and rot, is no longer in his chair.

I freeze. The chimes crash to the ground.

"Crap," I whisper.

"Zoe?" Will calls from the yard. He comes forward and leaps the three porch steps in one stride. "You okay?"

My blood rushes in and out of my chest with painful speed. I kneel down and scoop the chimes into my hands, methodically untangling the thin wire that holds the dolphins and rods in place.

"I'm okay. Just, he's not in the living room."

This knot won't unravel under my shaking fingers. Come on. *Please* release.

Will passes by me and looks in the window. "Probably in the bathroom." He puts his hand on my elbow and tugs. "Let's get out of here."

Before I am able to straighten up, the porch light goes on, bathing us in yellow. We stand still as statues, as though that would make the light go back off, make my dad go back to sleep.

The door opens. He shuffles onto the deck, a nearly empty bottle dangling at his side.

"What're you doin', Zoe?" he slurs, squinting at me. My breath comes too fast for me to be able to answer. My heart pumps in my chest in short, staggered movements. "What th' hell's he doing here?"

My dad points his bottle at Will. I close my eyes, willing my dad back to sleep. Will's grip on my elbow tightens.

"Git off my property, boy, or I'll call th' cops," my dad says through gritted teeth and phlegm-filled throat.

"Yeah, we're leaving."

I stumble forward because Will is tugging on my arm, but it's hard to move past my dad without flinching.

"She ain't going nowhere with you," my dad says. He reaches for my other arm, his fingers burning tentacles wrapping around and around my wrist.

"Let go." My voice is weaker than I want it to be. That is always the case around my dad.

"Let go of her." Will tugs again.

"Hell I won't," my dad hollers into the night.

I snatch my arm from his grasp, tumbling backward from the strength of my movement. Will and I push forward, hopping off the porch and into the overgrown lawn of weeds and grass. We're halfway across the yard when the bottle hits me square in the side of the head. I can hardly believe he could have such great aim in his state, but there is no doubting his determination to bring me down. The glass doesn't break but makes a sickening thud that I hear twice, once outside my head and once inside.

I fall to my knees with a surprised cry and put my hand to my face. I can't see. There is blackness, then there are flashes of red and yellow. I blink, hard. Move my jaw round and round. Will says something to me, I feel his hands on my chin, but I can't see him through my blurred and flashing vision. My wrist trembles, gives out under my weight. I fall, face-first, into the crabgrass.

Will leaves my side, runs for the porch. I can hear them, growling and snarling at each other like bears. When I finally roll over onto my side and take in the scene, I scream for him.

"Don't, Will, don't!" He answers me by plowing his fist into my dad's gut. He connects again, this time his knee with my dad's forehead. "Stop it, Will!"

I struggle to my feet, trip and coat my knee in grass stains, get up again. He will kill my dad. He can endure the way the old man treats me even less than I can. My dad slams into the wall, and Will balls up his fist again and punches him in the jowls. I see the red glisten of blood on Will's knuckles, but I don't know if it's his or my dad's.

"Will!" I scream. "Will! Stop!"

I buckle when a sudden wave of nausea hits me. I watch my dinner fly from my mouth and into the grass. I spit, cough, and gag, run for the porch. My hands shake uncontrollably. My legs hardly carry me. Pain sears through me.

My dad waves his arm backward, reaching for the door, a way to escape. A moment later he is on the ground. Will kicks his ribs once, twice. He will kill him. And my dad hardly deserves less.

"Stop, Will," I rasp. I reach him and grab his hand. He spins on me, his eyes lost to me. I step back, trembling, needing him to return to me.

"Zoe."

Will pauses to give my dad one last dirty look, then lifts me into his arms and carries me across the grass. I tuck my body into itself and press my palm to the side of my head. He starts to stutter as he suddenly sees himself the way I was seeing him, with familiarity, but the wrong kind.

"Zoe. Zoe. I ain't never gonna hit you. I ain't him. Ain't gonna be like that. Ever, Zoe. God, don't look at me like that. I'm not the monster. I'll never do what he did to you. I promise."

I uncurl myself out of my defensive position and press my forehead against his shoulder, against his salty neck, sweaty from exertion, inhaling the scent of him, which almost drowns out the disgusting flavor in my mouth. When he sets me down next to his car, I lift his hands and press his bloody knuckles to my cheeks, hoping they mark me like war paint.

"Let's go, Will."

Will opens the door for me and I slide in. I look to the porch as Will starts the car and turns the headlights on. My dad lies on his side, blood dripping from his nose, the sticky red mixing with whiskey and snot, and watches us go.

WILL

"YOU SMELL KINDA, LIKE, SICK," I TELL HER.

"That's because I puked on the lawn."

"Are you sick?" I squeeze my hand on the steering wheel and twist the leather cover. I need this tsunami of energy gone now, but the anger hangs on like a stray cat you've fed once and don't stop coming around. "Sh— Zoe, that's a sign of a concussion, ain't it?" I look over at her once, twice. She seems tired, all leaning against the passenger-side door. "Hey, don't go to sleep yet, 'kay? Here, drink some water. But don't sleep. I think you're supposed to stay up for a while."

I stop watching the road. She swishes water in her mouth. Rolls down the window and spits. I pull her face toward me. I check out her temple but don't see too much in the glow of the headlights. Not that I know what I'm supposed to be looking for. I wish I did know. I wish I knew something useful, anything. I rub her jawline with my thumb and swear. The tires hit shoulder gravel. I face back to the road. She moans at the swerving motion.

"I'm sorry. Sorry. Just, don't go to sleep yet."

No, she ain't supposed to sleep. But I want her as comfortable as possible. I jacked a couple of extra pillows and blankets from the supply closet at the home when I left earlier today. Figured I deserved more of a going away present than the boot to my ass I got from the state. Once we've sped out of the town limits, I reach into the back of the car and grab a pillow and blanket.

"Here," I say. "Put the seat back and relax. Give it, maybe, another hour before you go to sleep, though. I'm just gonna drive for a while."

"No, I want to stay up with you all night," she says, smiling at me a little. A forgiving Zoe smile. Guilt's my new best friend. I shouldn't have attacked her dad. I shoulda held myself back. But I couldn't help it. I'm so damn tired of seeing him beat the shit outta her. Her face is all fucked with the swollen lip, the nasty bruise under her eye. And she can't never fight back. She won't hit him back, never. She needs me.

Zoe studies the pillow I handed to her. "Is this yours?"

She figures I stole it. No, I ain't gonna let that bother me. She's right. I got a grand burning a hole in a paper bag under the seat to prove it.

"We had extras," I tell her. "Don't worry about it. There's a whole closet full of these things. Brand-new stuff. All bought with your tax dollars. Don't worry about it."

Zoe laughs at me. It's gotta hurt to laugh, her head's gotta ache and her lip, too, but her smile is amazing. It lifts everything. Even me.

"I've never paid taxes. Never allowed to work, remember?"

I downshift as we approach a stop sign. Roll through. There ain't no time to stop. Who knows what's chasing us.

"I remember. And you're not gonna have to, understand? I'll take care of that when we get to Vegas. I'll find work. I can do anything. And I'll take care of the bills. Your job is to finish school, get your diploma or get your GED or something and go to college. You're too smart to end up like me. Like, stupid."

She wants to be a nurse, she'd told me a bunch of times. The kind that delivers babies. I can't remember what she called them. Some word that didn't have nothing to do with babies. I feel her hand over mine as I shift up again.

"You're not stupid," she tells me. Her voice is soft. She soothes me. And I believe, for this split second, that I could have a future worth something, too. That's what she does to me. It's the most amazing thing.

"Oh! I almost forgot."

Zoe unbuckles her seat belt and twists around to the back of the car. I tell her to be careful, peek over my shoulder. She rummages around in her makeup case, then comes forward again and settles into her seat. She's got a lump under a napkin in her right hand and a lighter in her left. I look back to the road while she flicks the lighter.

"What's that?" I ask her.

"Hang on a sec." The vapor of the lighter fluid fills the car. "Okay, here you go." I look again. And grin. Can't keep cool 'cause she holds out a cupcake to me, with one candle in the center. The cupcake has a swirl of some ugly-ass blue frosting and a handful of sprinkles on top. "Happy birthday," she says.

It's nice hearing her say it. Last Friday, she snuck out and met me at the beginning of her street. We drove to the quarry. Charlie and everyone from the home—even Shelly, 'cause she likes a party even though she's supposed to keep us straight—sat around drinking cheap beer in my honor. When Charlie saw us coming, he raised his can and sang the usual too-old-for-the-system birthday song: "Happy Getting Kicked Off the State to You."

I wanted to deck him. Wasn't something Zoe needed to hear.

Zoe squeezed my hand and shook her head when Charlie offered her a beer.

Later, Shelly's all yammering to Zoe about all this money she's got saved up to buy a house, and Charlie grabs me, nodding in their direction.

"So, Torres. What are you gonna tell Zo' when you go?" He laughs. "That rhymes. Zo', go."

I shake my head and toss my empty can in the quarry. He's an idiot.

"Damn, you just gonna leave? I didn't think even you'd be that cold."

I raise my fist and he flinches. I've beaten him up for less than this before. "Screw you, man. It ain't like that." Shelly's still going on about her savings.

"It's not like she can go with you. You can't even take care of yourself."

"Shut up."

He rubs his face on his sleeve. "Jesus, man. You gonna try and take her? She ain't even legal." I don't say nothing. His girlfriend's barely out of diapers. "Fuck, man, you learn anything? You can't save girls like that."

"She's not like us." I clench my teeth.

"What? 'Cause she don't live in the home?"

"Shut up, Charlie."

"Cause she's smart? Pretty? She's as fucked-up as anyone else. Hey, you banged her yet? Better do it before you go."

I leap to my feet and kick Charlie in the ribs. He falls over with that drunken mix of coughing and laughter. I grab his shirt and lift him to his feet.

"Shit, man," he slurs.

Shelly runs over and grabs my arm. Zoe stands back, staring at me. She should look disgusted, but it ain't like that. She looks patient. I don't get that. 'Cause she's seen this stuff a million times before? I drop Charlie on the gravel. Go to Zoe. Her eyes dart from me to Charlie. He'll be fine. I take her hands.

"Hey, don't. He's wasted." I smile, trying to shove down this feeling like I gotta hit something. I tilt her chin to me and look her in the eye. "I got to thinking. You should come with me."

She looks surprised. "You're not going to stay and finish school? It's only a few months until you graduate."

"You're the only one who thinks I could do that." She don't know how good it feels that she thinks that. Even if it ain't true. I'd have to do summer school to redo the stuff I messed up.

"I can't just leave." She says it like it's a question. Suddenly, this idea I just started to have is the best I've ever had.

"You can. Don't you want to get outta here? Don't you want to get away from your dad? People who don't care about you? I care about you." She licks her lips. "We could go anywhere, do anything. I'm gonna get— I got money and you got brains. We could go anywhere," I repeat.

"It's too crazy." Her voice is quiet.

"What've you got here? What's here you can't leave?" I start to walk away from everyone else, pulling her with me.

"Go right now?"

I laugh. "Just walk with me."

We walk around the quarry and I talk and can't shut up like . . . this idea keeps coming 'cause it's too good to stop. I can see us driving away. I can almost feel the freedom. She gets excited, too.

"Like, Vegas? We could go there. See the Strip, all the lights in the middle of the desert. Do anything we want." I stop walking. "I'll take care of you. You know that?"

Her eyes flicker in the moonlight. She wants this. She wants someone, finally, to take care of her. Make her the best thing in their life. I cup her face and kiss her before she can think too hard about why she shouldn't do this.

I kissed her a hundred times before taking her back to him that night. She blushed and hid her eyes every time I touched her lips. I didn't take her home until she said she would come. But she never said happy birthday then. It's nice to hear it now.

"Hey, that's so sweet. Here, let me—" I lean over and blow out the candle.

"Did you make a wish?"

"I didn't have to. Look at us. My wishes are coming true."

I can't see it in the dark car, but I know she's blushing. She's the type who's gonna blush at everything.

We pause at a stoplight. I check the rearview mirror. Empty roads. Keep my hand on the stick, never let the wheels stop all the way. Go.

"Hey, you ran that red light!"

"We got places to be."

She laughs like it's a game and peels away the wrapper around the bottom of the cupcake, then passes it to me. The frosting tastes much better than it looks. But she's cooked for herself and her dad all her life. She knows her way around a kitchen. She even tells me what to do to my ramen dinners to make them taste like real food. Add chicken and vegetables and healthy stuff. 'Cause she cares that I got good food. It's nice.

I pull off onto the shoulder of the road and let the engine idle so I can finish my cupcake. I'll give a minute for Zoe's cupcake. But my eyes are on the side mirrors the whole time.

"Want a bite?" I offer her the last piece, but she shakes her head. I shove it in my mouth and kiss her before I've swallowed it all. She don't mind when I get frosting on her lips. She licks it off. "Thank you," I say, brushing her hair away from her face.

"You're welcome."

I kiss her again and accelerate back onto the highway.

I don't know what time I was born. It's on my birth

certificate, in that folder I was given on my way out. I might be eighteen by now. It's after eleven. I probably am eighteen. But birthdays don't matter much to me. All I've gotten today was a reminder not to take anything that don't belong to me and a chorus of "good lucks" from the rest of the cases back at the home.

And a cupcake. That's the best thing. Maybe my birthdays will be getting better from now on.

I look over at Zoe, flexing and unflexing my knuckles. They're not too sore. They calloused over a long time ago. She's nodding off on the pillow, but I'm wondering if I should keep her awake. I gave her my own pillow, so she could get used to the smell of me or something. So she can get used to sleeping near me. To sleeping with me. Her neck's exposed and I want to kiss it. There's things I want to do to Zoe. I wonder if she thinks about that like I do. If there's stuff she wants to do to me.

It still amazes me sometimes that she's here. But she sticks by my side, thinks I can do something with myself. I ain't never had a good birthday, until this one.

"Zoe, baby, you shouldn't sleep yet."

"Mm-hm," she replies.

I dart glances at her. Check the rearview mirror. Check the road just long enough to make sure we're still on it and not heading for some ditch filled with cow shit. I know she's not gonna be able to stay up all night with me. We're two different creatures that way: she has the brains and I can stay up all night.

"Stay awake a little longer," I repeat. I grab her hand and press it to my lips. She smiles all tired like. "Tell me about what kind of nurse you want to be again."

She talks for a while as I drive. Tells me about wrinkly babies and about dads who pass out in delivery rooms. I laugh at that. I would probably be like that, too, someday, all crazy overwhelmed by becoming a dad and all the blood and stuff.

I figure my own dad didn't hang around long enough to experience that. I don't know my dad, but I do know that my mom was on her own when she gave birth to me. After two years she figured it would be better for her to dump me off at her neighbors' and never come back.

"Wanna know something?" I ask when she stops talking for a minute. "I think a baby that looks just like you would be beautiful."

Zoe leans across the parking brake and kisses the corner of my mouth.

"Can I sleep now?" She yawns noisily. I check the dash.

"It's been, like, about an hour. You think that's long enough?" She should know. She's the one who wants to be a nurse.

"I think I'll be fine. I'm not dizzy or anything. I think that's what you have to look out for. Wake me when we get to the state line, okay?"

She pushes and pulls on the pillow, shaping and testing it three or four times before settling in. I tuck the blanket around her with one hand. It's hard to keep my eyes on the road. She is so sweet, dozing off in my car, lying on my pillow.

"I'll wake you when we get there," I tell her.

ZOE

IT'S BEAUTIFUL SLEEPING IN HIS CAR. I'VE NEVER SLEPT
anywhere but in my own bed in my own room. Unless you
count the times I blacked out on the floor. But I don't think
of that as sleeping.

It's not a deep, constant sleep, because even though my
body wants to rest, my brain doesn't. It wants to be awake
with Will, watching what we're passing, looking back at what
we're leaving behind. Feeling the touch of his hand on my
neck, hearing his steady breath next to my ear.

Sometimes my body wins, and I doze. I dream about
lying next to Will in ways we never have before, feeling

the heat of embarrassment mixed with nervous longing as I sleep; but other times my brain wins and I wake drowsily and ignore the pounding in my head to play with the fairy song of my mom's chimes or to smile at Will and put my fingers on his cheek. He's handsome to me, in his rough way. I've always thought he was handsome, since the day he transferred to the home and, later, to my school.

Being in the home gave him a ready-made group of people to hang out with. He spent that first day walking the halls with Charlie Harmon, who graduates this year and plans on going into the army, and Lexi Simon. She's two years younger than Will but dropped out a couple of weeks ago when she found out she was pregnant.

He commented on the bruise on my forehead that day, an unfamiliar voice floating out of a group crowded around a couple of lockers, and I tripped over my own feet.

I suppose everyone else in town was used to seeing them. The dark marks I tried to cover with makeup. I figured I had been doing a really good job, because nobody said anything when I showed up with some new disfigurement. But then this guy I'd never met before walks up and talks to me and he makes me doubt everything I thought I believed.

I guess it was just a case of the old stain on a hidden part of the wallpaper. When you see something often enough, it becomes invisible.

But it's okay now, because Will saw. He came to visit me

after that. At home—but only one time, because my dad told him to get lost—during lunch, after school. Sometimes he snuck me away in the middle of the night under a secret-keeping moon.

In a handful of weeks he's become my new belief.

This night is the black kind of dark when there is no moon and it's hard to see the houses we pass only every ten minutes or so. But I can see the stars if I lean forward and look out the top of the windshield. The stars don't seem to move, even though we're flying down the highway. There are always lots of stars in this part of North Dakota. They crowd in sympatheti-cally, as though they can't bear for any place to be completely deserted. As if aloneness scares them, too.

"Will, do you think there will be this many stars in Las Vegas?"

He looks at me for a long time before answering, and I feel my face flush with heat. He smiles at me, his easy smile, and looks back to the road.

"Sure. Stars are the same everywhere, ain't they?"

That doesn't sound right, so I laugh at him and he laughs back, but I don't contradict him because I can't put my finger on the right answer, either. Something about the hemispheres, but it's hardly worth taking the time to remember right now.

"If there ain't, I'll get you some of those glow-in-the-dark sticker stars to put on the ceiling, okay?"

I blush again because suddenly I'm thinking about the

apartment we'll share and the room we'll share and the bed we'll share. We've been together for almost two months now, but he's never put a hand out of place. I think he's like that because he respects me. I hope so, at least. But sometimes I wonder about his hands out of place, and the thought of it brings heat to my cheeks.

"Sounds good."

I doze again, dreaming of greenish sticker stars in the sky. Will wakes me up when we're about to cross into South Dakota, and I search for a Welcome sign. It's my first time out of my home state. Not for Will, though. He was born in Nevada and made his way here by little hops and moves throughout his life. He tells me I'll like it there, even though he left when he was four and probably doesn't remember Nevada. He wants me to like it because . . . I think we're going to be there, together, for a long time.

I believe him—that I'll like the desert, the Southwest— because he never lies to me.

I expect there to be more excitement as we cross into South Dakota. And maybe there are more lights, but the road is still quiet and lazy. I can't figure out why Will keeps checking his mirrors, jittery like we're in the middle of some big-city rush hour. I see the sign, and my heart quickens for just a moment before I settle back into the serene darkness.

"That was it," I whisper to the window.

"We shoulda brought confetti so you could throw it out the window. Or a camera."

It feels a little as though he's making fun of me, but I push the discomfort aside. Of course he's not making fun of me. Just teasing a little, maybe. I can do it, too.

"Yeah, but that means I'd have to teach you to use one."

"It's just pressing a button."

"*And* pointing it. That's two things at once. I'm not sure if boys can manage that much."

"Ha!"

He pulls his cell phone out of his pocket and aims it toward me, flicking on the car light at the same time. I hear the click of the camera and he turns the phone around so I can see myself on the screen.

"There. Now you got an 'Entering South Dakota' picture."

I study the face on the phone. The tired eyes, the swollen lip. The new shadow on my temple. I close my eyes against it. This is what Will sees. He sees it when my face is naked, when I have my makeup on: it doesn't matter. This is what he sees when he looks at me.

"I look awful."

The car swerves so abruptly that my seat belt locks as I'm thrown to the right. We hit gravel and he slams on the brakes. I worry that I've made Will angry when he gets out of the car, slams his door shut, and comes around to open mine. He unbuckles my seat belt and pulls me out of the car.

"You. Are. Beautiful." His arms are strong and tight around me. Desperate, even. "Don't ever say you're nothing but beautiful, understand? This—" He touches my lip, my eye. "This will fade and your heart will heal and you'll never have to worry about hiding nothing ever again. Understand?"

Tears spring to my eyes under the intensity of his gaze. I tuck my head into his chest to avoid his eyes and burrow against the softness of his shirt.

"You're so beautiful. No one's ever gonna hurt you again."

I nod.

"I'm so excited for this. For this life."

"Me too," I whisper.

"Okay."

He moves aside the pillow and blanket so I can get back in the car. He tucks me in again, even though I'm too warm. I'm warm even though it's early spring and still coat and hat and mittens weather. I reach my face up to kiss him, long and slow, and my skin is suffocating under the blanket. Will puts a knee on my seat so he can better reach me and spreads his hands on my face. They are like a brush of night breeze against my skin.

"Amazing," he says once he's pulled away. "You." He says it like he means it, and I have to believe it's the truth.

He closes my door gently and returns to his side of the car. He gives me a smile and another kiss and pulls back onto the highway.

WILL

I LOVE THE TASTE OF HER.

Sweetness and a little bit of acid.

Alive and warm.

It's the most delicious taste ever. It's been hours since she was awake, and the sun's practically up, but her flavors are still right there. Right in my mouth.

The gas tank thing's on *E* and has been for a few miles now, but if I stop for gas, she could wake up. If I stop for gas, they might catch up. Her dad. Shelly. The cops. I'm waiting for them, but I'm also waiting for that free feeling, that one where my fingers don't shake and I ain't gotta keep looking over my shoulder. When does that come? How far I gotta travel for that?

I know there ain't a whole lot of gas stations in this corner of the world, though, so I gotta stop at the next one. She stirs when I pull off the highway and slow the car. I creep to the pump, like she'll adjust to the changing car speed if I do it real slow.

Her breathing changes. She's waking up. I wrap my fists around the steering wheel and grit my teeth. Like it's so much to ask that I could do this one thing right.

"Sorry. We need gas."

"It's okay," she whispers.

"You need anything from the store? Are you hungry?"

She shakes her head.

"We'll stop at the next diner we come to for breakfast, okay? I'll just grab some water for now."

She nods and rests her head on her pillow again but doesn't close her eyes.

I feel her watching me as I walk into the 7-Eleven and grab a bottle of water. I feel her watching me as I pull two twenties out of my wallet, for the gas and the water, and toss them to the clerk. I don't look at her when I walk back to the pump, but I'm smiling 'cause I can't help it and now it's a game. She wants me to look at her, I know it, and I wanna tease her instead.

I try to wipe the smile off my face and look cool, but I don't got much control in the Zoe department and she sees it. She always got to me, stripped my bullshit down with a look. Charlie never missed a chance to tell me I was whipped.

I still ain't looking at her, even though I can hear her laughing at me. I clear my throat real loud, set the latch on the gas pump, and pop my head in through my window.

"Okay, you win."

"Yep."

"You always gonna win at this game."

"Yep."

Her eyes are bright and all crinkly at the corners when she smiles like that. I'm gonna make her smile like that all the time.

I stifle a yawn, and her smile slips a little.

"Don't worry about it. I ain't tired. Just need something to drink." I break the cap on the water and chug half the bottle. The cold goes right to my head. Burns inside my chest. But at least I feel awake again.

"I can drive," she says. "You'll have to teach me. But it's not like there's any patrol out here."

I hesitate before answering her. Look around, sweep the gas station parking lot. The roads. Like the cops'll show up just 'cause she said their name.

I nod. She should learn to drive. She needs to, and this would be as good a place as any to teach her. Plus, it's the perfect excuse to give her the ID I got made for her. I'll tell her it's for driving, and not 'cause she's fifteen and I'm eighteen and I don't wanna get screwed when someone finds out I'm with this girl in another state. There's rules about that. I know that shit.

I open my wallet and look at her ID. It looks good, made from her yearbook photo, with the ugly white background. It should look good. It cost enough. I pull it out and close my wallet. I look at my car, and I look at Zoe. My car's pretty much all I got, but it ain't worth as much as she is.

The gas pump lever clicks off.

"All right. Gas station guy says there's a town with a diner about thirty miles up the road. You can drive there. I'll be all right once I got something to eat."

She's all excitement and happy squeals and I suddenly want to pull her out of the car and kiss her until she makes more of those noises, but for me, not the steering wheel. But I turn back to the pump instead and screw the gas cap on.

"Let's get away from the station before I let you in my seat. If you hit one of these pumps you'll blow us all up."

"Ha-ha."

She's clutching her seat all bouncy-happy, and my chest swells, 'cause that's me who did that. I made her excited.

When we get a mile down the road, I pull off onto the shoulder and trade places with her, passing the keys off when we meet at the front of the car. She dangles the keys in my face with a laugh and hops in.

ZOE

"DON'T KILL ME," HE MUMBLES AS I SLIDE INTO THE
driver's seat. I sock him in the shoulder. Then I kiss him
because I feel bad. When I pull back, he pats the car with
exaggerated sympathy, looking at me sideways the whole
time, and I don't feel so bad about the punch anymore.

"Here."

He passes me a card and it's my face staring back at me.

"I probably should already have one of these," I say. "I
mean, a real one. When did you get this made? And . . .
eighteen? Wow. I don't—I don't think I can pull that off."

"You'll be fine. You're mature. And it's only a couple of years. You *look* legal now."

"To drive? I only have to be sixteen for that."

"Yeah." He looks over his shoulder for a second. "And, you know, to do whatever you want."

I follow his gaze, seeing nothing but desolate land in the space behind us.

Whatever I want?

"Um, that sounds good to me. Doing whatever I want." I shove the card in my jeans pocket. "Now teach me to drive this bad boy."

He looks back again, laughs. I grin in response.

"Okay. That pedal on the far left is the clutch. You gotta push that in when you start the car and when you shift. Do that with your left foot. Use your right for the brake and the gas."

"At the same time?"

"No, not at the same time. Do you want to stop and go at the same time?"

"No." I snicker.

"The brake's in the middle and gas's on the right, the narrow one, there. Put your foot on the gas when you wanna go. On the brake when you want to stop. The car's in neutral right now, so go ahead and try starting it up. Remember, push the clutch in when you start it up."

He's so nervous and trying so hard to hide it from me. But

he can't relax in his seat and it's so funny that I can't get the key in the ignition because I'm giggling too hard.

"Push in the clutch!" he barks.

"What clutch?"

"On the left."

"What's a clutch?"

"It's the—" He stops when he sees the look on my face. "Okay, know-it-all. You do it. I'll just sit back and enjoy the ride." He doesn't sit back at all. It doesn't seem possible, but his back gets stiffer. And it takes an act of supreme willpower to steady my hand enough to insert the key in the ignition.

I press my foot against the clutch, a little surprised at how much effort it takes to get it to the floor. Then I turn the key.

The car growls to life beneath me. I feel it trembling in my legs and arms, and I shiver with excitement.

"Put your right foot on the brake."

I follow Will's instructions because now that the car is alive I feel an overwhelming sense of responsibility, like the car is a child depending on me. I need to get this right.

"Okay, first gear is up here. You'll start there. Once you got it in gear, release the clutch slowly and press on the gas at the same time. Slowly."

I cover the gearshift with my hand and his covers mine and I shiver again. I look at him, catch his intense expression, and completely forget his instructions. I'm doing this. *We're* doing this.

We shift into first and I press on the gas.

Slowly. All the way down.

The roar of the engine comes so fast and so loud that I yank my foot off the clutch. We fly down the road, thrown into the backs of our seats, until I shriek wildly and pull my other foot off the gas. I cover my face with my hands as the car instantly halts with a shriek and tosses us forward like rag dolls.

It's silent.

"Oh my gosh. I'm so sorry," I whisper.

He's laughing.

"It's all right. I think you left the transmission back there, though." Will turns in his seat and studies the road behind us. I'm sticking my tongue out at him before I think about how childish it is. But he doesn't think it's childish. He grabs me and tugs me to him, across the stupid stick shift, and finds another use for my tongue.

I'm loving this freedom to kiss Will in his stalled car on the middle of a highway in South Dakota. I clearly remember the first time he kissed me. He'd caught up with me as Lindsay and I waited for the bus the day he came back to school after his suspension. He didn't say anything—just took my hand with a mischievous smile and tugged me away from the curb.

Lindsay giggled at me when I remained flat-footed, pulling back against the force of Will's insistence, not knowing what to do. I knew I wasn't supposed to go, that I would deserve the trouble I'd get into if my father found out. "I'll cover for you," she said. She gently pushed me toward Will. I bit my lip.

"My father—"

Will made a dark sound and wrapped his arm around my waist. His touch sent the breath from my lungs; heat rushed up my neck, into my cheeks. No one had ever touched me like this before, with the surety of wanting to touch without hurting, and now Will had, twice in a row.

I craved his certainty.

We hurried to his car just as the bus pulled up to the curb. He unlocked the passenger door with a sweeping gesture, and I laughed at his gallantry as I climbed in. I reached over to unlock his door, then paused, realizing that I was sitting in Will's car. I'd never been in a boy's car before. I took in the crumpled receipts littering the floor, the empty soda can in the center console, the scratches in the dash and fine-lined cracks in the seats. The interior smelled softly of worn leather and oil.

His shadow filled the driver's-side window. I froze, my hand somewhere between the steering wheel and the lock. He inserted the key in the lock, watching me through the window. I couldn't move under his dark molasses stare. My arms tingled. I swallowed and slowly dropped my hand as he opened the door and slid in with only a whisper of sound.

The car door shutting startled me, but he reached out

and brushed my bangs to the side.

"How come you wear them so long? In your eyes?"

The air was too thick—heavy—for my tongue to move. I felt safe behind them, I wanted to tell him. Even now, with my forehead exposed, I felt too open to the world, to him. His shirtsleeve moved up, revealing a tattoo that stretched around his biceps.

I touched it with the tip of my finger, then snatched my hand away as fire filled my body. I looked at the dash, the radio, anywhere but at him.

"I got that last summer," he murmured. "Worked on a ranch. They used barbed wire fencing to keep the animals from getting out. So I got that. Thought it'd help keep my animal from getting out."

I wasn't sure what he meant. He wanted to keep things in, and all I wanted to do was get out.

"When you look at me like that," he said, a little breathless, "it's like you understand things about me I don't even get. And you don't even say nothing. You're the quietest person I've ever met. And I know you're smart, so it can't be that you ain't got nothing to say."

"I don't have anything to say that really means anything," I whispered.

"I think you got so much to say." He leaned in until I could feel his breath on my lips. "You don't have to say it right now, though."

My pulse quickened, but I didn't move, caught in a moment of indecision. Do I let this happen or not?

He hesitated and tension washed over us. "I ain't never asked permission before," he said. "But is this . . . okay?"

His eyes flickered from my mouth to my eyes. My lips parted against my will, but I knew I was incapable of forming words. I nodded.

I watched him press his lips to mine, then dropped my lashes as I sank under a wave of warmth and sweet-salty taste. The scent of his car mingled with the musk of his skin. The silence inside the vessel enveloped us gently. He was soft, careful, so that all I knew was the press of his lips, the whisper-tickle of his breath, the tips of his fingers on the back of my neck.

A new craving.

When he pulled away and brushed my bangs aside again, I knew I would risk sneaking out a million times to kiss him again.

But now there's no sneaking around to avoid my dad, who hated Will from the moment he set eyes on him. He called him "bastard orphan." I'm not sure that makes sense, but my dad liked the name well enough. Will ignored it. He ignored everything my dad said and did to him . . . but not the things my dad did to me. There's enough hate for my dad in Will to create a life philosophy.

That's left behind now. Here, in this heap of metal, I can

savor Will's mouth, the crinkles at the corners of his eyes, the earthy smell of his warm skin close to mine.

"I love kissing you," I say as I scramble back to my side of the car. "But I'd also love to learn how to drive this piece of crap."

Will's hand flies to his chest and he winces at my words. "Shh, she didn't mean it," he murmurs to the cracked dash.

I'm still giddy from our kiss, so I jam one foot on the clutch, put the car in gear, and slowly trade the pressure on the pedal on the left for the pedal on the right. It's a trial-and-error kind of thing, releasing the clutch just right, while pressing down on the gas the same amount. But after a minute of very slow movement, I've got the car rolling down the highway at a respectable ten miles per hour and my foot is off the clutch completely.

"Okay, how do I go fast?" I press a little on the gas, but the revving noise doesn't sound right.

"You've got to upshift now. See that gauge, right there? That's the RPMs. You can watch the needle and shift when it gets to around three thousand, but it's better to just listen. Go a little faster. That's it. Hear how the decibel ain't really rising no more? Yeah, that's when you gotta shift."

I can hear it. I press down the clutch and put my hand on the stick. Will guides it into second gear.

"Nice job."

His praise lifts me, makes me feel like I could fly.

"You're a good teacher."

"Not so much, but I know a piece of junk like this old car."

He calls the car a piece of junk, and it isn't much to look at, but it means a lot to him. He saved up for two summers to buy the car and do the work it needed to run as smoothly as it does. I know he wants to do more, but that will have to wait until we're both working.

He guides my hand into third and fourth gears, and by now we're soaring down the road. It's exhilarating, like a first taste of real freedom, to be in control of a machine that can take me far, far away from where I've been. I'm enjoying the ride so much that I pass right by the diner we're supposed to eat at.

"Oops." I turn the steering wheel, but we're still going really fast and I don't know how to slow down. I can't take my foot off the gas, because I remember what happened last time, and braking would be pointless. I steer as hard as I can, putting my whole body into the movement. The wheels screech on the road, and I yelp. We're headed for a ditch. "Will!"

"It's okay. Use the brake and the clutch at the same time. I'll downshift."

It's too much to keep track of—the wheel and the shifting and the brake, the clutch, the gas—and my head's spinning and there's the ditch and my feet get tangled under the dash.

I've got the clutch but forgotten the brake or the other way around, but as we slow, I hear a nasty grating sound and see Will wince again.

"The clutch, baby."

My hands are gripping the steering wheel like it's a life-saver. I take a breath and try to focus on the pedals. The clutch goes in and I'm turning the wheel for all I'm worth. The car's slowing down, but not fast enough. "Will!"

He leans over and takes the wheel. "Brake! Just brake!"

I slam both feet on the middle pedal, and we slide half-way into the ditch with a shudder. A shattering sound splits the air as a semi truck whizzes past us, horn blaring, driver's middle finger extended out the window.

I try to catch my breath. It feels like I've been running for miles.

"I'm sorry."

"No. You did great." His voice is a little shaky. "We'll try again later. But I'm hungry, so . . ." We get out and push the car back to the road. I'm useless because every time he lifts his arms to push, I get the urge to tickle his sides. We end up sprawled on the weeds, hands and mouths seeking, twice, before I am flushed and out of breath enough to leave him alone.

I want it to be always like this. Cars in ditches and tick-ling and kissing in the weeds because we can't help ourselves.

I never want us to be able to help ourselves.

WILL

I FIGURE I COULDN'T CARE LESS ABOUT MY DAMN CAR.

She's there driving it into the ditch and I start to get more scared that she's gonna hurt herself than I am about the fender getting smashed up. But then that passes and we're okay and the whole thing's way too funny.

It's a good thing she tickled me. I don't want her to think I was laughing at her driving.

It's sunny. Still cold, but definitely morning when we get to Sullivan's Diner. There's enough cars in the parking lot to tell me that this's the joint to eat at in this tiny town. I take Zoe's hand and hold the door for her when we walk in and wait to be seated. We sit next to each other in the booth. Her leg presses against mine and I feel it in every bone of my body. I clear my throat and pick up the menu. Someday she's gonna figure out what she does to me. Pretty soon I'm gonna let her know what she does to me.

When the waitress comes, Zoe orders oatmeal and I get eggs and bacon. The waitress pauses for a sec and looks over Zoe's face, but Zoe don't even notice. Her brown eyes are hidden by a curtain of dark hair. But those bruised-skin colors ain't easy to miss. The waitress looks at me with raised eyebrows.

A volcano erupts inside me, fire and suffocating black ash, and I want to take that waitress outside and show her what I ain't never done, would never, ever do to Zoe. But Zoe hears the butter knife I'm clutching rattle against the table and looks up and sees what's going on. She glares at the waitress until the bitch walks away with a huffy breath.

We don't say nothing about it.

Instead, I rub Zoe's arms 'cause she's still wearing her coat and I'm worried that she's too cold. The Dakotas ain't exactly warm sunshine and blooming flowers in April.

"Do you need anything? Want me to grab the blanket?"

"No, I can't sit here wrapped in a blanket. That would be way too embarrassing."

"There ain't nothing you could do that would embarrass me."

She gives me a smile and snuggles into my side, but she don't change her mind about the blanket.

"Do you think I could waitress in Vegas?"

I squeeze the saltshaker in my fist. We'd gone over this already, a couple days ago, when we started mapping out our escape.

"No."

"That sounds a lot like you telling me what to do."

"You asked."

"I have to do my share, Will."

"You will. You'll go to school. That's your share."

"What about money? It costs money to live."

She would know about that. She had to get to her dad's Social Security check each month before he did so she could cash it and pay the bills. She told me about how Lindsay's dad waited at the end of Zoe's street the day the money came to give Zoe a lift to the bank. I asked her how come Lindsay's dad didn't do more. She shrugged. People mind their own business, she said.

I hope they do. I hope they keep out of ours.

"I told you, I'll find a job. I got lots of work in me."

"But I want you to finish school, too."

I shrug. Someday, maybe, I will. But it takes a lot more effort for me to do schoolwork than her. I just wasn't made for studying and raising my hand in class and all that sort of thing. I was made for honest labor and there ain't anything

I could figure I wanted to do with a degree anyway, so that's fine with me.

"Will."

"We'll take turns. You go to school first, 'cause you're so good at it. I'll work, 'cause I'm so good at that. When you're done with school, we'll trade." It's a simple solution coming out of my mouth, something so she'll stop talking about this. But inside, something else is building up. Something bigger. I whisper it to her so it's out there, so it ain't nagging me no more. "I will go to school, Zoe. I want you to be proud of me. I want you to want someone like me by your side. And I'll do whatever it takes to earn that."

She shifts against me and I feel her lips on my neck, right at the spot that's tightened up. I'm glad the waitress shows up just then so that I can focus on the smell of our food and not the weird tightness in my chest. I grab the ketchup and dribble some on my eggs.

"I have raisins," Zoe says in this happy-girl voice. She pops one in her mouth.

"That's cute. But I've got manly food." And I lower my voice to sound like Tarzan or something. She snickers. I know she loves it.

We eat without talking for a few minutes. Her jeans are pressed to mine and I wanna show her what she does to me—right now—but I got to focus on something else, like the sound of bacon as I crunch it between my teeth.

When I've finished my breakfast and she's halfway through her oatmeal, I pull the map book from next to me and show her the roads we're gonna travel to get to Vegas.

"See? We're on the eighty-three right now. We'll follow that for a ways longer until we hit the two-twelve."

"How long till we're there?" she asks.

"Another couple of days, I guess. Depends how much we drive each day. You in a hurry?"

She shakes her head. "Every minute I feel more and more free. We can go slow, I don't mind. It just draws the nice feeling out even longer."

"Yeah." I feel the same way, but I've never been as good as she is about just saying it. Her honesty catches me off guard.

I shove down the yawn that's creeping up and reach for my glass of ice water. I'd figured the food would wake me up, make me more alert. But I'm getting more tired than before. Crunching the ice between my teeth helps. The cold's painful on my teeth, but at least I feel awake. I kiss her on the top of the head.

"Cold."

"Sorry."

"Don't be," and she kisses me on the lips. Her mouth is burning hot over mine, but I hold the kiss until I'm as warm as she is.

"It's gonna be good when we're a little farther south, though. Get a change of scenery, feel like we're actually getting somewhere." She blushes and I nudge her. "What?"

"I'm slow. I'm holding us up."

"Nah, you're fine." I'm pretty sure that ain't why she's blushing, though, and I'm dying to find out what the real reason is. I always wonder about what she's thinking, what she sees when she looks at me, how she feels when she's with me. Her expressions and her actions don't hide much, but I can't help it. I want to know it all. Make sure I'm doing the right thing, saying the kind of stuff she needs to hear.

I don't get girls like I should, I guess. Didn't have no sisters, didn't have a mom. Wasn't the sort of thing I could learn from the girls at the home. Those girls didn't know normal, either.

"Let me know if you need anything."

"Yep."

I sit and smell her hair while she finishes eating. It ain't a perfumey smell, or fruity, like coconut or nothing, but something in between. A smell I could get used to.

"You got, like, shampoo and stuff? Everything you need?"

Her cheeks turn pink again, and I can't figure out what I've said that made her blush this time. This whole "taking care of someone else" thing ain't something I'm used to. I spent most of my life looking out for me, moved from foster home to foster home until I was finally put in the group home. I didn't get close to nobody. You never could know when your new foster parents would be drunks or crazy or . . . you know. Or when the other kids were more fucked-up than you were. So now I gotta try and figure out how to not be in her face too much but still be supportive enough. I feel like I never learned where the line is. It's just one more thing I got to figure out.

"Just tell me if you need to stop for whatever, okay?"

"I will."

The little bell above the door tinkles. I look up. Then down again. Zoe eats her oatmeal like nothing's happened, 'cause she ain't noticed. She's gotta hurry up.

Look up.

There's two of them and, yeah, there's the car with lights across the roof out the window, at the corner of the parking lot. The waitress ain't got to them yet. They're still standing in the entryway.

"You almost done?" She looks guilty.

"Sorry. I'll hurry."

I sink down in the booth. "No, it's cool. Didn't mean to be mad."

She looks where I look and drops her spoon. The cops shift their stances like they're impatient. Or looking for something. My stomach clenches.

"Don't look at them," I tell Zoe.

"Do you think—"

"Nah. Gotta be cops around these parts, right? It's okay."

I fumble with the saltshaker. "It's probably the only place to eat."

"Let's go."

"It'll look bad if we just go. And we still gotta pay."

The waitress comes out from the back. Grabs two menus. Small talks. Walks this way. I sit up, pick up my fork. They ain't here for us, I know it, so why's my blood racing? Shit. Don't look up. Don't look.

They approach.

I look up. Lock eyes with the younger one. Do I look guilty? He'll know that I shouldn't be here if I look away.

Shit.

I swallow and nod. Zoe clatters her spoon against her bowl, and that cop, he's gotta know something's up. His hand goes to his belt and I'm ready to bolt. He nods back. Slides into the booth behind us.

Zoe makes a sound.

"It's fine," I tell her.

"I'm done eating."

"Wait just a minute."

"We have to go."

"Hang on. It can't look rushed."

The waitress slips us our bill on the way back to the kitchen. I grab it.

"Let's go."

ZOE

HE GOES UP TO PAY THE BILL AND HE LOOKS SO COOL, but I'm shaking as I stand in the aisle between table and booth and watch him pull money out of his wallet. I'm trying not to look at the police a few feet away. Why had I never thought someone would come after us? Stupid, naive girl.

The waitress takes the bill, and Will eyes the pocket of his wallet as though counting what's left. The only money we have is what was left after he bought his car. I don't know how much that is, but I can't contain the guilt I feel that he's paying for everything. I have to contribute somehow.

"Ready?" His voice is clear and his eyes a forced bright.

"I can try driving again, once we're far enough away from the police."

He laughs, then quickly pulls me into a hug to hide it.

"I don't think so. Let's just get on the road and get some loud music on. That'll help. We'll stop when it's warmer and take naps, 'kay?"

He wears a T-shirt like it's warm already. I run my hands over his bare forearms, mottled with moon-shaped scars whose history I don't know yet. His arms are lean but strong, and I suddenly believe he can take care of everything. Even half asleep. Even if we were being chased.

The loud music does help. Especially since it's loud rock music and Will doesn't know the words to the songs. That doesn't stop him from singing at the top of his lungs in his enthusiastic but tone-deaf voice, though.

"*. . . if a braid weight should fall . . .*"

I choke on a sip of water.

"That's not how it goes!"

"*. . . runaway with my horse . . .*"

"Wrong again!"

I laugh even harder when he bites his lip and waves his fists in the air during the bridge. His black hair flops around his face as he moves to the beat and his warm eyes glitter.

"No! That's so embarrassing!"

That makes him dance harder, shaking the car with his

movements. He rolls the window down and sticks his head and shoulders out.

"I'll go wherever you will go, Zoe Benson!" he yells to the wind.

"Get in here!" I grab at his shirt and try to brush away the tears that are streaming down my face at the same time. The car swerves and I shriek-laugh, but I couldn't care less if we head into a ditch for the second time today.

"Anywhere you go!"

"We might not get farther than this field with the way you drive," I say when he finally brings himself back into the car and snatches my hand for kisses.

"Doesn't matter, baby. Long as I'm with you. You make me do all kinds of crazy things."

"Oh, I do not make you bite your lip when you dance."

He grins at me and I think maybe I could get used to watching this psycho dance like that.

It's cold, but I roll down my window, too, and surf my hand up and down the drafts. My hair whips around me, but I don't care. I don't care that my lips are drying out or that my ears are stinging. I suck the air into my lungs and the pain is blissful. I feel like I could reach my whole body out the window and let the wind carry me to wherever Will wants us to go.

By early afternoon he's completely worn-out and even the water and music aren't helping.

"We could get a Red Bull or a coffee or something," I suggest as his eyelids fall and the car slows for no reason other than that he's forgetting to press on the gas.

His eyes snap open like he has something to prove. "Nah, I saw a sign for a rest stop a couple miles ago. It should be coming up here in a sec."

When we come to the stop, he pulls off into a parking lot surrounded by short, golden-brown barrenness. We step out of the car and stretch and use the bathrooms. I bring a change of clothes in with me and wash myself as best I can with abrasive powdered soap and wet paper towels. It's not much, but I feel slightly less grimy when I return to the car.

Will is already there, leaning on the hood. I walk into his outstretched arms.

"You still good?"

"Yeah."

"Listen. About that ID. You're gonna want to tell people you're eighteen, if they ask."

"Why?"

"Why? 'Cause you ain't supposed to leave the state without a parent."

"When you say 'not supposed to,' do you mean something bad could happen? Maybe we shouldn't—"

"Nothing bad is going to happen. Don't worry about it."

He kisses me, slow like we have time that doesn't exist

for anyone but us. I tuck my fingers up under his shirtsleeves and trace the armband tattoo there. I pull away and kiss it, all the way around his arm.

"I don't wanna sleep no more," he says into my lips as he brings my face back to his. He lifts my legs around his waist and turns so that my back is against the chilly hood. I shudder, but from what he's doing to me or from the cold, I don't know. It doesn't matter. All I know are these tremors in my belly and how glad I am that he pulled me off my feet before my knees could give out on me.

My head is spinning like a dust devil, and his heat is closing in on all sides, surrounding me until I'm breathless, but I have to get control of it or he won't sleep.

"Will," I gasp.

"Mmm."

"Will. You have to sleep."

"You taste like rainbows."

Laughter bubbles up from the depths of my belly, and Will pulls away with an irreverent grin and a hungry glint in his eyes.

"What? And what do rainbows taste like?"

"You. So good." He grins at me and I push him back.

"Get in the car, dork."

"Always with the name-calling. Hurts my feelings."

"I'm sure."

He must have emptied the stuff on the backseat to the

trunk while I was in the bathroom, because it's all clear now except for a pillow. He moves the front seats as far forward as they'll go, climbs in, and tries to arrange his frame in the limited space.

"Come sleep with me," he says, patting his chest invitingly.

"There's not enough room."

"Sure there is. Come here."

I climb in, ducking down into the tight space. He draws me on top of him.

"It's cramped back here," I murmur, sinking into his body.

"It don't matter. I want you all over me, taking up every inch of space around me."

He breathes it so close to my ear that his lips are a brush of goose down on my lobe. It sends my body awash in shivers. I can't get close enough. He smells good, and he's so warm. I'm tingling all over and I want to keep him awake longer, be more important for him than sleep, but I know I can't. He should rest.

But I need to hear his voice.

"Will, what did you want to be when you grew up?"

Everything about him smiles: his mouth, his closed eyes, the palest shadow of stubble on his jaw.

"A baseball player."

I sit up a bit in surprise.

"Really? I didn't know you played baseball."

He pulls me back down and cages me with his arms.

"I never have. None of my family ever wanted to spend the time and money Little League takes. By the time I got to a decent foster home, I felt stupid asking about it, so I didn't. But I did swing a bat once, when I was thirteen. This family that had just taken me in, the dad was trying to get into his kid's room in the middle of the night. She'd put her dresser in front of the door and piled up her clothes and stuffed animals like they could be her army. He made a ton of noise, but nobody came to stop him. Who wouldn't— There was an old bat in the backyard and I grabbed it and sent the old bastard down the hall with one swing."

His shoulder twitches as he remembers the swing. "It felt good to hit him. Me and Aubrey—that's his daughter—we got taken out of there the next day."

"I bet you saved her a lot of pain."

"Don't know what good it did. If I asked what happened to her, they told me it weren't none of my business."

He brushes the bangs out of my face and kisses my nose. I settle into his chest; his arms wrapped around me are heavy and tight, like the smell of my dad's Jack. But I hated Jack and I think I love Will.

WILL

I SHOULDN'T HAVE TOLD HER THAT. ABOUT AUBREY.
I never want her to be afraid of nothing, the way Aubrey was
afraid. Maybe I'm too late for that. Maybe Zoe's dad took all
of her fifteen years and taught her to be scared. I'll undo it.
Help her learn to be strong again. And brave. Not that I'm
any kind of example, but we can learn together.

I kiss her across her forehead. I'll wipe away the memories of her bastard dad from her mind. Help her be strong. I
promise her silently. Rest my lips at her temple. That promise
is the last thing I remember before I fall asleep.

My muscles groan at me when I wake. I'm too stiff to

move, and Zoe's gone from me. But there she is, just in the front seat. She turns to look at me when I grunt in her direction.

"Hi there."

"Why'd you go up there?"

"You were trying to move. Trying to get more comfortable, I think. I was in the way, so I came up here."

I sit up and my back's pissed at me. "Ugh. We need a real bed." She looks away for a sec, and I see the color and can't hold back a smile. I reach forward for her hair and twirl a piece around my finger. "You can pick out the furniture, 'kay?"

"Okay."

Outside the car I stretch and pop joints and moan a little. Blood begins rushing back into places I didn't realize before were missing it. Little pins stab up my ankles and calves. I try to shake them out, but I can't tell if it's helping or making it worse.

"Did you sleep up here?" I ask as I adjust the seat back to where I like it.

"No. I wasn't too tired."

"You just sat here?"

"I took a walk. I thought about stuff. Made plans and went over things."

I look at the ignition as I insert the key 'cause all three of those things sound dangerous and freak me out. But I don't want her to see that. She's a big girl. She can take care of herself, even on walks in the middle of nowhere where ax murderers could be lying in wait for unsuspecting girls to go out alone. And thinking's good. But making plans kinda messes with me. She's smart enough to make plans without me, but I don't want her to. I want to be a part of everything she does.

"What kinds of plans were you making?" I make my voice steady and cool. I'm not trying to smother her. That ain't right.

"I was thinking about school. How I need to finish. Can I do that with a fake ID? How do I fill out forms? I guess I get my GED somehow . . . and then college?" She plays with a dolphin on her mom's chimes while she talks. "What kinds of classes do I have to take? And about how I'm going to have to study a lot." She's holding the chimes up, making the dolphins swim. The sound's annoying as shit. "And how I want to sit next to you on our couch and study while you watch baseball. I want you to learn how to play baseball, Will." She drops the chimes and faces me. "I bet there's some league you could play in or a college PE class or something. I'll learn with you, if you want."

"Yeah, that would be cool." I can't tell her that there ain't no way I'm gonna get in front of people and not be able to hit a ball. I can throw, I guess. Even catch. But swinging at a white blur flying by my stomach seems impossible. Connecting with anything that comes at me fast ain't easy.

It's somewhere between lunch and dinnertime when we hit the road again. She surprises me by grabbing a bag down by her feet and pulling out a couple of apples, some crackers and cheese spread—the kind in crinkly plastic packages with the little red sticks—and a bag of frosted animal cookies with sprinkles.

"Where'd that come from?"

"I got it out of the trunk when you were sleeping. It was in my makeup case." She lifts her chin a tad. "I didn't pack my makeup."

Well, shit. Awe soaks me from head to toe like I got caught in the rain, and I'm reminded what a fuckup I am. I shouldn't have doubted for a second that she could walk around the rest stop on her own. I gotta remember that, let her be strong on her own, 'cause a guy like me ain't gonna fix her.

She cheeses up some of the crackers and hands them my way as I drive. We share an apple, passing it back and forth after each bite. We're both trying to take small bites, making sure there's enough for the other person.

I toss the core out the window. She pops a cookie in my mouth, but I ain't paying attention. There's a glint in the rearview mirror.

I gotta take another look 'cause I ain't sure what I saw. She gives me another cookie, but I can't remember finishing the first one. I bite. The sprinkles pop under my teeth. I look again. There's something glinting on the roof of that SUV behind us. I can't tell what. Not yet. It might be rectangular. Too far, but I ain't slowing down to let them catch up. I ease the accelerator down, pick up speed, build space between us. I check the side mirror and hope that car ain't really closer than it appears.

"Slow down, Will. You're going to get pulled over."

"Everyone drives fast out here," I tell her. Like the SUV. Where the hell are they going so fast?

I get a good look. The car's white. White and something across the top. Shit. I floor it. The engine revs. We're flying and Zoe's scared. She's got one hand clutching her door and the other one on the dash.

"Will!"

But we gotta move or we're screwed. I check the stretch of highway. Check the mirror. Why ain't he got his lights on? The gap's opening. I'm pulling away. I hold the wheel so tight sweat forms on my palms. Fields rush by, and if I lose control we ain't stopping for a long time.

There's a town coming up, the kind of place where I gotta slow down, go twenty-five. I push one last time, gain more road in between us. Another look back. The SUV's a square, hard to even see the lights. It slows, turns off on some back road. I take my foot off the gas.

Hunting lights. That's all it is across the top.

I relax my muscles. Push my head back. Zoe gives me a look.

"Just testing her out. See how fast this baby can run."

Zoe lets her hand fall off the dash. "Boys." She laughs.

I ain't sure she believes me. I should tell her about the money. No, not yet. Not till we get to Vegas and she realizes we need it. Any sooner and she's just gonna think I'm a thief.

My heart slows down as the car slows down, and I figure we're okay, I figure I shouldn't overreact like that. But reacting quick's just the way life made me be. Ain't never felt safe much.

Zoe leans on my shoulder. She watches the fields and nothingness pass us by.

I check the mirrors.

ZOE

THERE'S NOTHING, REALLY NOTHING, OUT HERE. Acres and acres of graze land and wheat land and who-knows-what-else land. At this time of year, though, the land isn't being used for much. Just sitting, waiting, resting. Brown and going on forever.

We slow when we pass through towns. I brush my finger distractedly across the bottom of my chimes when we're tired of the radio but need more noise than the ever-present rush of tires on road. Sometimes the glittery sound makes me think she's here, escaping with me.

We look curiously around those small towns, as though

trying to see if this was the kind of place we could see ourselves living someday. But the towns are all small and we're
sick of small towns. We can't ever go back to places where
everything is everyone else's business. Everybody's business,
unless it's something really important. Then everyone has the
right to ignore it.

In first grade, Mrs. Hilliard spent two days a week
running the school library. She saw things, asked a lot of
questions, until the day my dad walked into the principal's
office wearing an American flag T-shirt and his "I'm a vet"
face, shouting at the principal to mind his own business. Mrs.
Hilliard kept her lips zipped from then on, but she never
stopped watching me, an ever-present shadow hanging over
me as I browsed the shelves or curled up in a corner with
Little Women.

She retired at the end of the year and volunteered at the
public library. Whenever I went there, she'd ask how things
were at home, would sit with me for a few minutes, telling
me about my mom, about how she was a student when Mrs.
Hilliard first started at the school library. She said I looked
like my mom. The same eyes, the same mannerisms. I was
just like her, she'd say. She always made it sound like it was
a good thing.

"What do you remember about Nevada?" I ask Will. He
extends his arm over the back of my seat and shrugs.

"Not much. It's hard to remember much about where

I've lived. I don't know. Bushes? And the mountains. It was northern Nevada, so not in the flat desert or nothing. There was snow in the winter."

"I think I could be happy never seeing snow ever again." There's a long season of snow in North Dakota. It's not so bad when you're let out to skate and play hockey. But it makes for a crappy six months of the year when you're stuck inside all the time.

"Yeah. Vegas probably don't get snow."

"Probably not."

I kiss the inside of his elbow. And blush. It's funny how some big moments, full of kissing and touching and everything, don't make me embarrassed, but the little ones do.

I've asked Will about all the places he's lived before. He lists them off, one by one, as though he's recounting someone else's history. Nevada, then some time in California. At one point his grandma, his mom's mom, tracked him down and took him to live with her in Colorado. That was one of his worst times. She liked to put her cigarettes out on anything that moved. The cat, the TV screen, Will. When she died, an uncle took Will to Nebraska and tried to make a man out of him by locking him out of the house at night, just because.

Because you're a man if you can fight off a coyote at the age of ten.

His uncle's wife, a decent woman, Will says, took him

with her when she fled to North Dakota. They lived in a one-bedroom apartment for a few months. Will was by himself most of the time, since his aunt worked day and night, but after everything else, it was a blessing to be left alone.

Then she met a guy who didn't want kids around, and Will went to the state.

I told Will once that I was grateful for the way my life was. At least I didn't have to move all the time. At least I knew a couple of people, people who talked with me and ate lunch with me most days. I had Lindsay. Even Mrs. Hilliard, who remembered things about my mother I never knew and set aside books she thought I would like. The teller at the bank who didn't care that I signed my dad's name on his checks for him when I went to cash them. Will gave me a weird look when I said those things, like he couldn't believe my experience had been better than his.

But I never went hungry for days, waiting for my aunt to get home, and I don't have a parade of little round scars on my forearms like he does.

"Hey, how far is Vegas from California?"

"I don't know. Pretty close. Here, check the map." He pulls the map book from under his seat and I set it across my lap, flipping pages till I get to Nevada. I press my finger against the dot that is Vegas and another against the border and bring them together. I check the scale and make an estimate.

"Yeah, it's really close. A couple of hours, maybe? Let's go there sometime, okay?"

"Definitely."

"I want to see the ocean. And the stars."

"They're probably the same stars like everywhere else."

I laugh. "Not those stars. The ones on the sidewalk in Hollywood. And the place where actors have their handprints in the ground."

"I didn't think you were into all that stuff."

"I'm not. But it's Americana, right? I mean, we're supposed to do things like that and take pictures and say we've been there. I want to say I've been there. I want to do it all. See the Statue of Liberty someday. Disneyland. Other countries. All of it."

"Okay, we'll go. Some weekend after we get settled in. We'll go to Hollywood. And the ocean, too. Promise."

"I'd like that."

I've never actually owned a swimsuit. I've never set foot in a pool, and I don't know how to swim. I'd probably run screaming if I actually saw an ocean wave, but that doesn't mean I don't want to go and see what happens. It might be nice to discover something scary in a way I'd never known before. The heart-racing, in-love-with-the-risk kind of scary. Not the hide-away kind.

"Can you swim?" I ask him.

"Yeah. I lived in an apartment that had a pool. The

complex, I mean. I learned one day."

"In one day? Wow."

"It was either that or drown. I got pushed in by this neighbor guy one time. I was playing on the concrete with a Tonka truck and he just ran up and shoved. Jeans and shoes and all. Thought it was funny to dunk the kid."

"It doesn't sound funny." I see a little Will, falling into the water, splashing, clamoring for help. He cries out, he chokes. I close my eyes against the image.

"Nah, but at least I learned to swim."

WILL

ONE OF THE PROBLEMS WITH DRIVING A FORTY-YEAR-old muscle car is that gas ain't cheap no more. We're a couple hours into Wyoming when I pull off to fill the tank. It's late and I figure twenty-four-hour gas stations will disappear in this part of the woods. Or plains. There's a sandwich shop in the convenience store, so I pass Zoe a twenty and she runs in to buy dinner while I pump.

The sky is cloudless. The air sharp and cool. The wind is picking up, blowing dust and gas fumes my way. I squint against it, try not to breathe too much, and look toward the store. Zoe's second in line and there are two guys behind her.

I watch them carefully 'cause one of them's wearing a denim jacket over his flannel and, I don't know, denim jackets rub me the wrong way.

They're talking about Zoe.

I don't think Zoe even realizes it.

How come she don't notice? Why hasn't she learned to be suspicious of everything? I wipe my hand across my forehead. I hate that. That she don't watch out for things better.

They're standing a couple of feet back, but their hands and their eyes and their words are all moving forward, toward her. They laugh and shove each other. I grip the gas pump like it's one of their thick necks and hiss.

One of them taps Zoe on the shoulder, and she turns, her eyebrows raised. Her lips form the word, "What?" The guy who didn't tap Zoe is smirking. What's he smirking at? What's he even doing touching her? The other one, the one in the denim, gives her a smile and a flick of the chin.

Zoe gives them a half smile and goes to face forward again when the guy asks her a question. She answers, politely. She's a nice girl. Nothing like me.

The guy says something else and Zoe blushes.

She blushes.

I yank the nozzle from the car and slam it back onto the pump. Gas leaks onto my hand. I'm watching them as I screw the gas cap in place and close the cover. They're laughing again and I know Zoe can hear it. I can hear it from here.

Her back is rigid now. Arms crossed. Shoulders square. What did they say to make Zoe blush? Bastards. What did they *say*?

I walk toward the store with long strides, and the customer in front of Zoe is taking her food and walking away. Zoe drops her arms to move forward, to order our dinner, when the guy in denim grins his filthy grin at his friend and slaps Zoe's ass.

Son of a *bitch*.

I'm going to knock out what's left of his rotting fucking teeth.

I rush the doorway 'cause there's nothing else in my line of vision. No cars, no pumps, no landscape going on forever. All I can see is the doorway and the woman before Zoe coming out and how I'm going in and the shithead's denim jacket, which I'm going to rip off and suffocate him with.

Denim jacket.

I reach for it, the jacket. The guy's shorter than me, not by much. But he's got at least thirty pounds on me. Don't matter. A wolf can take down a buffalo if it needs to.

He swears when I lift him off his feet. The jacket makes his arms, his shoulders scrunch up into his chest. He looks like a beetle, all flailing arms and legs.

"You need help?" I seethe and spit my words into his face. "You need help keeping your hands off girls? I got help for you."

I say something else, but I don't know what. Maybe it weren't even real words, just noise. I hear Zoe, and I feel the guy's friend grabbing at my arms. There's some other shouting, too. It's noisy around me, but inside there's clarity. It's just me and Denim Jacket's wild eyes. I set him down long enough to draw my arm back and connect with his trembling mouth. He sprawls to the ground, clutching at his face. He's soft. Thirty pounds more than me but it's all soft.

His friend is different.

His fist hits my ribs before I even see the punch coming. The air flies out of me but the rage grows. It's shoving and clawing at me like it wants to burst from my belly and eat everything around me. I see Zoe right behind the guy, grabbing his arm, and I'm furious that they did this to her, that she's being pulled into this mess.

Denim Jacket's off the ground now, but he's within range of my foot, so I kick his lower back and he falls again. There is a force, a blow, to the side of my head. I stumble back, become friends with the chips display. I feel the crunching of the bags under me and a boot to my knee. I grit my teeth against the pain and grab the guy's leg, yanking him to the floor. The sound his head makes as it hits the ground is so satisfying.

There's a shout and a noise like a backfire. Everything goes deathly still and the three of us are staring at the wrong end of a hot rifle.

"Get out," the rifle says. "Get out. Mosely, I'm charging

you for this mess. 'Cause you can't keep your damn hands off what ain't yours. But you"—I see an eye move from behind the rifle and fix me with a devil's stare—"get the hell outta my store. And take that damn girl with you."

Zoe wraps her hands around my arms and we bolt out of there.

Denim Jacket grins and wipes his bloody lip as we make our escape.

It's warm in the car, warmer than usual, but my chest is even warmer and my head's fucking on fire.

Zoe reaches for my cheek when we get inside. I jerk away, swearing when my knee connects with the dash. "Don't. What the hell?"

"Don't what? Are you okay? Is your knee okay? Can you drive?" She reaches for my leg. I swat her hand away.

"I'm driving now. See me driving?" I'm so pissed about this whole thing. "Were you flirting?"

It ain't what I meant to say.

I meant to ask if she was all right.

She freezes.

"What?"

"Were you *flirting*?" Dammit, I can't keep my mouth shut. I can't control this other person inside me that makes me shout stupid, angry things.

"Don't yell at me!"

I try to calm myself, but I'm like a boulder rolling toward

a cliff, picking up speed as I go, and ain't no stopping until I fall off the edge.

"Why were you talking to that guy? What'd he want? You just stood there and *let* him do it!"

Her arms are folded like she don't want me getting close to her, and I can't stand that, so I shake my head as though that can shake the anger outta me and hold my hand to her, move to get close to her. My voice is strained on the outside, but I'm hot, bursting bubbles and pleading on the inside. Be sorry. Don't be angry. Be sorry. The sorry ass that I am. My hand's in the air. Just there. Like, I want to reach for her and touch her face.

But I go too fast and I don't know what it looks like to her until she does the worst thing ever.

She flinches.

Suddenly, I ain't mad at her or at some guy or anyone or anything at all but me.

I'm like a boulder, rolling out of control. Until I fall. Or until she catches me, cradles me in her palm.

"No." The word chokes out of me like there are a million other words I gotta get out, too. "Zoe, no, God, I'm sorry. I'd never. You know I'd never." And I'm dropping my hand to hers and pulling it to me, worried that I'm holding her too hard or shaking her or squeezing her too much or something, anything that could hurt her. "I'll never do that," I tell her knuckles.

"Let go of me, Will. You're scaring me."

I drop her hand under the blow of her words and ram my head back into the headrest. I wince at the pain in my spine and put my hands on the wheel where she can see them, where she can see they ain't gonna do nothing wrong.

"I'll never hit you, Zoe."

Her eyes are softer now, liquid and cinnamon. She's looking at my cheek. I know it's bleeding and I want to wipe at it, so she ain't so worried about it, but that would mean I'd have to take my hands off the wheel and see her flinch again. I won't. I'll cut them off first.

"I know you won't. It wasn't that. Not really. But . . . you have to understand, Will, I . . . I see him when you're like that, is all. My dad. Will, you were so angry."

She says it like she's the one who's got to say sorry, like she did anything wrong at all. I close my eyes, shut out the road, tell her that I ain't her dad, that I won't never treat her like that.

That I'm sorry.

This anger-person: he needs to go away before I destroy us both.

ZOE

THEY SAY YOU END UP WITH THE MEN WHO ARE JUST like your dad. Right? That you're psychologically predisposed to picking an alcoholic or a cheat or an abandoner, or something like that.

I always thought psychology was weird.

I'm thinking this; at least I think I'm thinking this, but I'm not. I don't realize I've said it out loud—the part about choosing men just like your dad—until his groan reaches my ears. It's a cut-up sound, full of regret and hopelessness. He pulls off the road and stops the car. He buries his hands in his hair and slams his forehead against the steering wheel.

"Don't say that," he whispers.

I watch him some more. Watch his fingers clutch at his hair. He's making a noise of some sort, a dying animal kind of noise.

"You're not like my dad," I tell him.

But I'm not sure how I can make him believe it.

I can't believe I jerked back from Will like that.

The fear is too big. Bigger than me. Is that it?

How does a person stop being afraid?

My dad spends most of his drinking time in his chair, staring at the TV and laughing at the dumb shows. But when something sets him off, he's up fast as a cat getting its tail stepped on.

It can be anything, really. Me, dropping a cake pan in the kitchen. Political commentary. A fly in the house. The unpredictability means I'm never ready for the attack.

In his chair, he's fragile and white-haired . . . short, a wasted kind of thin.

It's a different creature that emerges when he's angry, but still, all I can see is that old man with a limp and a self-congratulating smile when he guesses the *Wheel of Fortune* puzzle before anyone else.

I suppose that's why I can't fight back.

That, and a genetic weakness. Mrs. Hilliard always said I was just like my mom. I used to think she just meant my eyes or hair color. How we both had soft voices. Now I wonder if it was something more she was always talking about. That we're both too weak to run from the monsters that chase us.

I put my hand on Will's cheek and draw him to me.

"Will. You are not like my dad. You don't want to be that kind of man. But he . . . he didn't care what kind he was."

He's cut on the side of his face. It's not bad, but it's enough to tear my heart open. None of this would have happened if I had just stood up for myself. Walked away, told him to leave me alone. Something. Why couldn't I have just done something?

"Will."

I want him to look at me, and finally, he does. His eyes have so many colors in them, green and gold and brown. And they're searching me for permission for it all to be okay. I brush his hair back and kiss his chin and then kiss his cut. I come away with the flavor of minerals, like water from a pipe gone bad.

"I love you, Will."

He whispers my name and presses his forehead against mine.

"I love you," I tell him again, because right now I'm filling up with him. Filling up with how hard he tries and how much he cares about me and how much he wants to save me. I kiss him again and again, hummingbird kisses, until he catches my face again and slows me down. He leans into me until our chests are pressed together and his leg covers mine.

I put my hands on every part of him I can reach and I don't want to stop.

But my stomach rumbles at us.

Will laughs and it's the most beautiful sound. It diffuses every bad thing between us and leaves only the good.

"You need some food," he says as he settles back into his seat and pulls onto the road.

I suck on my lips. Revel in the memory of the taste of him.

I'm sure he could sustain me.

Maybe Mrs. Hilliard didn't have it quite right.

Maybe I'm more like my father than she gave me credit for.

Maybe I'm as desperate for a certain flavor on my lips as he is.

WILL

THERE AIN'T NOTHING OUT HERE. NOWHERE TO STOP
or grab a bite or nothing. That's okay by me. I couldn't eat if
I wanted to. It's been a couple hours since we passed through
a fast food joint, since the fight, but my stomach's so heavy it
feels like I been eating nonstop for days. I'm tired, too. Tired
of driving and moving and fighting this thing that's drowning me. I know I should take care of Zoe, find out if she's
hungry again, but I don't know what to do if she is.

She faces the window and she ain't said nothing to me for
a long time and I don't want her to say nothing.

There's a pull-off, like someone started building a

driveway but changed his mind, so I stop and flip the head-lights off but leave the interior light on and get out. I know it's cold out here, my brain knows it, but my body don't feel no chill. I could stand here and freeze to death and never even know it was happening until hellfire thawed me out again.

What the fuck was I doing back there? Treating Zoe that way. Like she ain't the most important thing in my life. Causing problems. Do I want the cops to get called? Do I want someone to know where we're going? It ain't enough that I got one eye on the road ahead and one on the road behind?

There's too much to get us on. To get me on. I watched and waited until Shelly used her debit card in front of me. Until I saw her PIN number. Three days ago, I took her card. Took the five-hundred-dollar max for two days until the card wouldn't work no more. She figured out it was gone—the card, her money. I don't know if she figured out it was me. But we needed the extra grand to go with what I'd saved up.

Zoe still ain't legal, and it don't matter how bad she needed to get out of there—they're gonna call it kidnapping and theft, and if I'm caught, then we're both screwed. Run. Keep moving. Don't stop to get into no more trouble. Don't stop. Gotta keep telling myself that.

Keep going.

Keep running.

We got places to be.

I walk out a bit and pee in the dirt. It smells like cattle out here. Makes me wonder if there's a feedlot nearby. Just about the nastiest smell ever hangs around feedlots.

I get back to Zoe, shutting the door gently behind me after I get in, and try to smile all brave-like. 'Cause I got to do this thing for her. Show her something. That we're gonna get out of here. That I'm gonna be this better person she needs.

"I can do better."

She nods.

Nods the same way she did the first time I spoke to her. Back when I asked her if there was someone she needed me to take care of for her. I figured she'd laugh at me, but she nodded, all sad. I didn't think she would nod, but she did, and we just . . . connected. A zap kind of connection that I can't explain.

And I needed her after that. But maybe she don't need me like that. Like she'd be better off without me.

"You act like I'm perfect or something, Will. I'm not. I'm so messed up," she begins. I poke at the rearview mirror. Turn it toward her so I can see her talking to me through it. "You don't have anything to prove to me. I'm not going any-where. But you have to figure out another way to be angry. Or how to not get so angry."

"Don't you think I try? I try all the fu— all the time. It's like," I say, kneading the worn leather of the steering wheel. "Like, whatever I do, there it is, this . . . rage or . . .

something . . . that owns my blood and it burns . . . burns my blood 'cause it thinks it's funny or something. I just . . ." I grit my teeth, shake my head 'cause this shit ain't right. "And I get angrier and angrier and then . . . I gotta do something about it."

"You can't hit everything and think that's going to make it all better."

"I know that! But it feels good to just . . . stop fighting it and let it control me. Like . . . I don't gotta think none or decide or hold back or nothing." Zoe turns to me with this soft look, and it's pity, I know it's pity, but I don't care. She's here and it's gonna get better. "Everyone thinks I'm tough 'cause I fight. It's all over me like a disease, and it's easier to let it take over than to fight it. See, that's the fight I'm too weak to win. Get it?"

Zoe ain't even touching me and I feel her surrounding me like a blanket. I don't need this anger and I need her, but I can't let either of them go even though they're opposite each other. If I had her inside me like I have the rage inside me, I know I could beat it back.

"I feel like I been angry forever."

She takes my hand.

"I'm not going anywhere. Not without you."

"You know who's cared about me like this? Like how you do?" I bury my face in my shoulder so she can't see my shame. "No one. And here you are, and I'm screwing it up.

God, how can I screw this up?"

"You're not screwing anything up. And I don't care if you cry. I'm not going to think any less of you." She leans in close. Watches me. "We can't hide from each other."

"No. I don't—"

She waits, but that's all I got.

Then: "We'll get through this."

I nod. "Yeah."

ZOE

HE FOUND ME AT LUNCH. THE SIXTH DAY OF SCHOOL after winter break, the first day of Will. I'd hidden away to do Brain Bowl and he found me, bringing his group home buddies into the math room and just watching. Will told Mr. Hart he was thinking about joining, too, so the teacher let them stay.

All the other Brainers were nervous, intimidated by the foster kids. As though not having parents made them bad people. As though Will and Co. were planning on beating them up after lunch just for being smart.

But not me.

I got manic. I wanted to prove to this new guy who'd asked me about my bruise that I wasn't just some punching bag. So for every fry he ate, I answered a question correctly. And he stared at me the whole time, even when his friends were talking to him.

When we both realized it was a game, we shared a secret smile, and I had to stop myself from laughing so I could tell the teacher that Bratislava is the capital of Slovakia.

"You're smart," he said, waiting for me when the lunch bell rang. "I ain't never been smart like that."

I smiled and didn't say anything because my tongue was in knots and my heart was trying to escape my chest under his gaze. I knew I was turning red and I hated that. He was so cute, in a scarred teddy bear sort of way. Even I saw that, and I was terrified to read people for fear they would read me back.

"If you're so smart, why do you let people beat up on you? Your dad? Is that who does it?"

My smile froze and my insides froze, but my face blazed with heat. I walked away from him, stumbled around the first corner I came to so I'd be out of his sight.

He found me again during lunch the next day, in the library. I was doing chemistry homework and he was eating chips as he walked in, even though we weren't allowed to bring food into the library. That time he was alone. He sat in the chair across the table from me, shoved his chips in his bag, wiped his hands on his jeans, and stared. Again. I fought the self-consciousness that made me want to drag my bangs farther, longer over my eyes, over my entire face.

"They won't let you sand wood in here."

"You think I take shop? I'm that type, huh? I don't take shop."

"Yes, you seem like the type."

"Not since I sawed off Riley Mercado's finger last year."

I dropped my pencil. "Who?"

"At a different school. It was an accident."

I tucked my hair behind my ear and forced myself to think about science so I wouldn't start blushing again. *If a chemical system at equilibrium experiences a change in concentration, temperature, volume, or partial pressure, then the equilibrium shifts to counteract the imposed change, and a new one is established.* "I've got a lot of homework to do. And we're not supposed to talk in here." But I didn't want him to leave and I didn't want him to stay where he sat, either. I was mad at him. I wanted him closer. My equilibrium floundered as it tried to shift, neutralize, stabilize this unexpected disruption.

The confusion turned my stomach into a pretzel. No one had made me feel that way before.

"Want some help?"

"You've taken AP Chem?"

"You take AP Chem? Shit. Ain't you a sophomore?"

"It's an elective."

"So you *choose* to take that? Over, like, pottery or some other fun shit?"

"I like science. And I don't like cussing."

He shrugged. Hid a smile. "Okay. I'll give it a shot. How hard can it be?" He swung my book around toward him and glanced over the equations on the page. I watched his eyes move back and forth as he read and his lips as he mouthed the prominent words. His lips were perfect. I didn't notice when he stopped reading.

"I'm thinking the same thing," he said.

I tore my eyes away as a flush of heat crawled into my cheeks.

"What?"

"I wanna kiss you, too."

"I don't, I—" Indignation, like a simmering mud pot, mixed with my embarrassment, and I clawed at my book, slamming the cover shut on my finger. I cringed, at the pain and at the smirk I was trying not to look at. My pencil rolled off the table, but I left it on the floor in my haste to get out of there.

He didn't look for me at lunch the whole next week, but I saw him in the halls, and every time, he was twirling my pencil between his fingers.

Then he got in a fight and people suddenly realized I existed.

"You know that new guy? Will Torres? I guess he beat the tar out of Hank Prosser. Laid him out in the middle of the cafeteria," Lindsay told me. "People are talking about how Hank said something to him and the new guy just socked him, but nobody knows exactly what he said. Hank's, like, a foot taller than him and way bigger. But he went flat on his back."

People in the halls watched me and Lin when we walked to class. I stared back warily, wondering what they were thinking. Their eyes were so curious, it was like they were seeing me for the first time. Seeing the bruises, wondering where I'd been hiding the whole time. It was horrible being looked at, scrutinized. I wanted to scream at them to look away; no, I didn't want to make any noise at all.

"He hasn't even been here that long," I whispered to Lindsay.

"I know," she said, nodding. "They're going to ship him to another home if he's not careful."

"What did Hank say?"

She pursed her lips, then opened her mouth with a loud smack. "Well, everyone's saying he said something about you."

I paused. "Me? What could he say about me?"

Lin shrugged. "What is there even to say, you know?"

I stood in the center of the hallway, mouth agape, wondering why this new boy had to cause so many problems.

"Don't worry about it. It'll all blow over by tomorrow."
She gave me a quick, tight hug and dashed into theater as the
late bell sounded.

I left school at lunch and walked two miles in the freezing cold to the McMurray Home for Youth. I fretted over
what I would say to him, how I would voice the questions
he'd sown in me.

I wasn't much of a talker. I talked to Lindsay sometimes.
She'd ask, with an optimistic smile, where I was planning
on going after high school and the word "go" would bounce
around in my head in a million echoes, but I couldn't grasp a
single one long enough to analyze it or understand what the
term meant. Go . . . where? The guidance counselor brought
me into his office earlier in the semester to tell me about col-
leges and my excellent grades and other things, but I didn't
hear a word he said after he passed a stack of forms across
his desk, telling me to have my dad look over and sign them.
I'd given my dad papers to fill out for sixth grade camp years
before, and he'd promptly dumped them in the garbage.
Which is what I did as soon as I walked out of the counselor's office.

I always gave Lin a tight smile and said there was still lots
of time to figure out where I was going.

Everyone was going somewhere. The need to flee flashed
in their eyes as they walked down the halls, discussing playing football at Nebraska or vet studies in Washington. Envy

rushed to the surface when I overheard their plans, but the feeling dulled quickly, becoming tired and wilted around the edges when I realized I couldn't join in their conversations. I had nowhere to go. Besides, when I talked to other kids, they would make fun of me because I spoke like the books I read. Used words like "fretted."

It wasn't worth it. I stopped talking to people long before I'd figured out how to.

Peeling white paint and a plastic-patched upstairs window greeted me when I reached the group home. I knocked on the door, knowing my tongue would fail me.

He answered the door in boxers and a white T-shirt and with hair in his eyes. He looked like something from an underwear ad, but his eyes were sheepish when he peeked up at me, when he wasn't looking at the ground. My knees went weak and my voice was breathless with the only thing I could think to say.

"I heard they suspended you for a week," I stammered, the words growing a cloud of fine steam between us.

He took my hand and pulled me into the entryway, closed the door and helped me shrug out of my coat at the same time. He led me to a room with mismatched couches full of rips and Sharpie marks, and we sat next to each other. I studied his face, the shadow on his cheek where Hank must have gotten one punch in, and almost smiled at how we matched. Almost.

"Come here." He pulled me into his lap, knowing I would come, that I wouldn't say no. He held me, but he never told me what Hank Prosser said to make him send Hank to the hospital for seventeen stitches and a broken cheekbone.

He never would.

I look at Will across the car now and wonder, not for the first time, what Hank had said. And why Will won't tell me.

WILL

WE GOT MUSIC ON AND SUGAR HIGHS FROM DRINKING Coke when we enter Utah. The mountains are a nasty reminder of Colorado and pain that came quick and the smell of burning skin. But Zoe, who's read about everything and knows tons, is all impressed. She's got big eyes watching out the window. There ain't nothing to see but snowy trees and signs that tell you the elevation. But you don't go up where she comes from. It's so different from North Dakota that we feel like we've escaped everything by now. I gotta watch out for that. We can't get lazy. I adjust the rearview mirror and take a quick look, but the only things following us are a brown minivan and the mountain wind.

"Amazing. I understand that song now. You know, the one about America the beautiful? I'd always gotten the part about the grain. But not the purple mountain majesties. I get it now."

"Yeah, it's pretty." I guess it is, but Zoe gives me this look. She pulls on her straw with her teeth, and I clear my throat, check the rearview mirror for shadows. Three states down, two to go. We're fast. Faster than anything chasing us.

"Are we going to see the Great Salt Lake?" Zoe asks after she's swallowed her soda.

"I don't think we go by it. But we drive through the mountains for a while. Check the map if you want."

She checks and I ain't wrong. She's bummed enough that I almost change course and head into the valley. But she looks tired, too.

"How about we get a room for tonight?" I ask. "We can ask around to see how long it'd take to get to the lake and figure something out, okay?"

"I don't know if that's a good idea."

"Why not? It's gonna be too cold to sleep in the car. Don't you wanna sleep somewhere warm and toasty?"

I wait for her cheeks to flush like strawberries, but they don't. She looks worried.

"What?"

"Hotels are expensive." Her voice is low, like a shy child's, and she says this like she's scared. Like she ain't too sure how

I'm gonna react. I'm not sure I do a good job. She faces away from me when I look at her. I can't help it. I feel like she's poking needles in my pride, searching for the raw places and finding them with the tips of her weapons. I'm the man. I'm supposed to take care of everything.

"We can do a hotel tonight. I saved up. I got cash. A little room somewhere. Cheap. They're all over the place. Don't worry about it, Zoe. I'll take care of it."

"I know. I mean, I know you'll take care of things. But we have to be careful. Things get expensive, and the little things? They add up. We have to make sure we're okay for Vegas."

"It's one night. After this we get out of the mountains and it'll be warmer."

"I just don't think we should waste your money."

I downshift, holding the stick harder than I need to.

"It ain't my money. It's ours."

"I didn't earn it. You worked for it. It's yours, and some-day I'll pay you back."

I clench my jaw. Grind my teeth. I don't want it to be like that. Like me and my money, and her and nothing. I didn't work for nothing. I didn't risk getting caught with Shelly's card for nothing.

Why won't she take what I want to give her?

I reach for my wallet and pull whatever my fingers grab. I push it into her lap.

"Here. You wanna divide everything? This part's yours. It's a gift. Spend it however you want. Rest'll be mine. Work for you?"

I ain't looking at her, but she's quiet, like, sad quiet. She don't touch the money. I just want her to take it, to believe I wanna give her everything. I see it out of my peripheral vision, her hand swiping across her cheek.

Shit.

I gather the money and put it back in my wallet. I hold it out to her. She won't take it.

"That wasn't cool. I'm sorry, Zoe."

She nods.

"Let's figure this out now, okay?" I set the wallet in her lap. Try to be soft about it. "This money belongs to us together. That's what I want. You be the accountant person. Count the cash, make a list or whatever, like a chart, and figure out what we should be spending. You got that."

She nods and handles the wallet.

"You can do that? Like, you know how?"

"I can manage that. A chart, or whatever." She's smiling a little now. Good.

"I don't know what they're called. Like, balancing your checkbook, right? 'Cept I never had checks or a bank account or nothing like that."

"How did you manage to save up for your car?"

"I put the money in a box under my bed."

She's pulling out the money, counting it or something, but she stops when I say that and looks at me like I just said the most amazing thing.

"You stuck your money in a box? Like a *shoe box*? And no one in the house *stole it*? You're joking."

"It weren't a shoe box. It had a lock and everything. And everyone knew if they messed with it I'd beat the sh— crap out of them."

"Right."

"C'mon, you know everyone in the house. Just 'cause you get screwed over in life don't make you a crappy person. They were decent." I grip the wheel tighter. *They* were, at least.

"Yeah, I knew them. They had issues."

"So do I." I meet her eyes. "Hell, so do you."

She swallows and nods and looks back at the cash.

"Okay, so they were cool. But when we get to Vegas and you have a job that pays with a paycheck and not a fistful of twenties behind the tractor, you're going to get a bank account and debit card and everything."

"Long as you, like, monitor everything. I don't want to deal with all the numbers."

"Big baby."

She grins at me, so I grin back. Yeah, so I'm grateful she can crunch numbers so I don't got to. Big deal. Some people are good at that stuff and some ain't. I'll do other things, and put together it'll be good.

"So we're good for a hotel, right? I mean, the other option is freezing our tails off in the car."

"If that's the only other option"—she laughs—"I guess we'd better."

ZOE

THERE'S MORE MONEY IN HIS WALLET THAN I THOUGHT there would be. Money he wants me to think is mine, too. I have a hard time letting myself think that. Is it wrong to depend on him? It feels unnatural, frightening. But people who care about each other shouldn't feel that way, I know. It's just for now, I promise myself. Things will change. We'll be equal someday.

Large-denomination bills slide through my fingers, and I'm surprised that he's been able to save this much for so long. He must've been paid well, and I guess he never had much to spend it on. That, or he had a plan and was able to restrain himself so he could carry it out. I'm impressed. Because of that, and because I know the kind of backbreaking work he did at the ranch all day over the summers and on weekends and early mornings during the school year. He's not afraid to work. And he's not afraid of his plans.

I wish that were me. Not afraid. A worker. I've never been given the chance to be either.

The trees clear away after a half hour more of driving and we enter a mountain town, quiet at this time of night. Or maybe because it's a weeknight or because the ski season's winding down. Probably all of those things. Whatever the reason, I'm glad. Hotels will be empty and rooms easy to find, maybe even a little cheaper. Already I see Will glancing side to side, checking the vacancy signs and ducking his head to see the prices posted on the boards. We slow down to ten miles per hour as he looks.

"You just drive," I tell him. "I'll pick the hotel." I touch his leg and my fingers tingle.

"Sounds good, money girl."

I squirm inside at the nickname, even though I know he's teasing and hasn't given a second thought to the fact that I have control over the money. Holding Will's money—I can't think of it as anything but his, no matter what he says— makes me feel like an obligation with a high price tag, like I'm this thing he feels he has to take care of because it can't take care of itself.

Soon, I tell myself again. I'll make it up to him.

"Oh, hey! Turn around. That place looks good." I point to the right as we pass by a motel with a fake log cabin exterior. Will whips the car around right in the middle of the road and enters the parking lot. There are molting wood-carved owls keeping guard high in the corners of the building and splotches of half-peeled white paint in between the "logs." Like they don't get enough snow here and have to fake it.

"Thirty-four ninety-nine. We can do that."

"You want to stay here? What if the rooms are as bad as the outside?"

I shrug. "We just need someplace warm, right?"

"You, me, a bunch of bedbugs, maybe a dead body under the mattress. We'll all stay real toasty."

"Will."

"I just wanted it to be . . ."

"What?" Heat sears my cheeks. He catches my eye, and my breath falters.

"Nicer. For you. Like you deserve."

I swallow but can't think of anything to say. Not when he's looking at me like that.

"All right," he says. "Let's check it out. But if you itch your legs all night I'm shoving you on the floor."

We get out of the car and I wrap my arms around him with a giggle. "But you'll join me on the floor, won't you? You wouldn't leave me there all alone." I stick out my bottom lip.

"Uh, no." He pushes my lip back in and pecks my nose. "Unless you make it worth my while."

I pull away as he wiggles his eyebrows at me, take his hand, and lead him to the motel office. There's a moose head on the wall with a string of colored lights on its antlers and a middle-aged guy half asleep at the counter. He sits up straight and tugs his ski sweater over his belly when we walk in.

The guy looks us over and does this funny thing with his mouth where he sucks his teeth, then his lips, and pops them back out again. It's gross.

"Can we get a room?" Will asks.

"We take cash or credit."

Will shrugs and I hand him his wallet. He hesitates to take it, and I realize too late that I'm supposed to do this part. We're awkward for a second, testing out a dance neither of us knows the steps to. But I can't dole out his money like that, like I own any of it. I nudge his arm with the wallet and Will reluctantly takes it.

The guy behind the counter glances at our hands, not bothering to hide his disapproval at our naked fingers. He watches his register drawer open as he rings us up, as though he can't bring himself to look at us again.

"You two even legal?"

He holds out Will's change but doesn't let go of it until Will meets his eyes.

"Not your business, is it?"

"This is my property. Makes it my business."

"Yeah, well, don't worry. We're good."

He lets go of the change and nods, picking up the phone on the table to his left. He dials, but he's still talking to us, telling us about when he bought the place, about the lady who cleans the rooms. Will jams the money in his wallet and holds out his hand for the key, but the guy puts his hand up for us to wait. Will tenses.

"What's wrong?" I whisper. Will shakes his head.

We listen to the conversation, the owner telling the person on the other end that he has customers. Will turns away and I follow him to the door of the office. We look out the glass pane at the black street. There's a wailing sound, and the darkness is broken up by a flash of bright color.

"Get back, Zoe," Will hisses, pulling me away from the door. The sirens are louder. I watch Will's face, see the way his eyes run over the office as though he's looking for something vital. His jaw muscles tighten and relax and he pulls me close. We move back to the desk as the motel owner hangs up.

"Hope nobody's hurt," he says as he makes a mark in a ledger.

Will turns his back solidly to the door, but he watches over his shoulder. His hands grip my upper arms.

"So what brings you to the mountains?" the owner asks Will.

Will doesn't answer. He's listening. Listening to the sirens come closer, closer. What is he expecting? What is he dreading? Who was on the other end of the phone call?

Will shuffles his feet, restless. I place my hands over his and he startles.

"We're on our way to Vegas," I tell the owner. But my focus is on Will and the noise, so loud now. I wonder if the motel owner notices the way Will's muscles are taut enough to snap.

"Getting hitched, huh? Better off staying here and doing that. You know how many of them Vegas weddings go for broke? Too many."

Lights strobe through the office. We hear the engine noises mixed with the siren. Will pulls me closer. The owner turns to grab a key. There's a rush, one last high-pitched whine. A rattle of old door on an older track. The car sails past the motel and I'm awash in relief, giddiness. Will drops his hands from my arms and his breath rushes past my ear.

"Vegas wedding?" I repeat, trying to recall what the owner had said. "Do you have statistics for that? I'd be interested in seeing them." His assumptions grate on my nerves more than they should. I realize how nerve-racking the last minute was, how it felt like an hour. He raises his eyebrows pompously and sits back in his chair.

"I hear things. I see things. If you watched the news instead of MTV, you'd know about it, too. All those celebrities that get married there and divorce in a couple of months. Pay attention, girlie, and you'll learn something."

"I don't—" I begin, but stop myself, pursing my lips. I wouldn't put it past the guy to hold off on giving us our room key if I upstage him, and this argument doesn't really even matter.

He smirks as he passes the key to Will. "Room should be nice and clean. I called Heather just now to make sure. You kids have a good night."

I turn to leave, but Will gets directions to a twenty-four-hour Denny's before we exit the office.

"He was kind of a . . ."

"Get used to it. They're everywhere," Will mumbles, clutching the key in his fist. He's visibly shaken and I want to hug the tension away. "But there're more good people in this world than bad, right?"

"Like we'd know," I say, my worry for him making my words bitter.

His eyes flash. "Hey! Don't you start talking like that."

I rise up on my tiptoes and rub my nose against his.

Will takes my hand with a dubious laugh and checks the number on the key ring. "Five. Room five's right there. Here, take the key and I'll pull the car closer."

My first impression of the room is that it looks like something out of an old made-for-TV movie. Stocky pine bed and dressers without handles, a thin bedspread in a paisley print, and a Technicolor gold shag carpet grace the interior. I expect to see a mirror on the ceiling, but it's just cream-colored popcorn.

"Classy," Will says as he comes in draped like a coatrack with our stuff. "I like the sunflowers." He tilts his chin at the gold-framed poster of van Gogh's painting above the bed.

"It all matches your car."

"Ouch." He dumps our stuff in front of the heater and pads over to me, taking me around the waist and locking his knees for us both to lean against. "My car's a classic. Or it will be, someday, when I'm done with it. But this room? It's a dump."

"It doesn't smell like dead bodies."

"At least there's that."

We stand for a time, sorting the comfort from the nerves. His smell, his steady breathing, his arms are familiar and calming. The still air in the room, the bed, the expectations, they nag at the back of my skull and suck the moisture from my throat.

"Everything okay?" I ask. He nods.

"I wish I could sing. Or play the guitar or dance or something. Well, not, like, dance. I'd write you a song and play it for you."

"You don't have to write me a song. I'm impressed with you already."

He tucks his hands on the back of my head and rests his

mouth on my forehead. I close my eyes.

"I could stand here forever," he says.

"In this place? This oh-so-classy motel room?"

"That's the thing. It don't matter where."

There is silence in the room, thick as clotted cream. It bears down on us like it wants to enter our lungs and remove us to a place where the world would stay hushed and still just for us. I hear my breath, short bursts through my nose full of his skin and his clothing and his holding me.

My lips are at the same level as his collarbone, and I nuzzle under his shirt to reach the warmth there.

"We're gone," I murmur into his neck. "Free. We never have to go back."

"There ain't no one coming. We've made it this far. We'll keep going. We'll make it, as far as we want."

"I can't wait to find our place. Remember when you asked me to come with you?"

"I can't forget the way you looked at me like a little zoo animal, all hungry to get out of your cage."

I nip his skin, and his arms tighten around me. "That's me. The caged tiger-girl."

"I just wanna make you happy. And learn all about this tiger-girl you've been hiding from me."

I laugh and he pulls us down to the bed, where we lay on our sides facing each other. "And the first time I ate lunch with you?"

"Ate? You sat there staring at us like we were planning on roasting you for lunch. You didn't eat nothing."

"I was so nervous."

"I remember what your dad did when he found out you'd skipped half a day of school to see me."

"I don't want to talk about that. I don't want to think about that anymore."

"That was when I first figured I wanted to get you outta there."

"You hardly knew me!"

"There was just something about you. Like I've always known you. Like we've always been supposed to meet or something. Even if you don't believe in fate or soul mates or any of that stuff, I still feel like there's something."

"That's just lust speaking for you," I tease.

He drags me closer and throws his leg over my hip, wrapping himself around me like a blanket. "My lust has all kinds of things it wants to say to you. You wanna hear about it?"

"Long as it doesn't shout in my ear."

"I can manage that," he whispers as he touches my face and tucks me under him. "I can be soft as you want."

He brushes my lips gently, briefly, before pulling away. I'm surprised at this. I expected more. More kissing, more touching, more expectation and pressure. But he looks at me like I'm this precious gem he's just picked up off the ground and wants to pocket and keep. I love this look, though it makes me want to hide myself in his shoulder, under him, in a black hole.

It scares me. These things that I thought were real a week ago—feelings that felt so big, so overwhelming—now seem like they were a fairy tale, a little girl's imagining of her Prince Charming. But these moments, every second more I spend with Will, show me how flat, how untrue, the fairy tale is. How much better—and worse—real life is.

I want to kiss him. I want to not be scared.

I can't think of anything to say, so I make him talk.

"Was it all bad? Every home, all the time?"

Will releases me and settles on his back and pulls me along with him. He ponders for a while and I listen to the relaxed thump of his heart in his chest.

"Nah, not always. There was this lady, she was Sioux, and she did the holiday shifts. Like, she took the foster kids for a couple weeks at a time so the regular parents could get a break from us. Keep their sanity or whatever. Anyway, I went to her twice a year for a couple years and she was cool. She liked to tell us all her tribal history and get all pissed about the white man. We all got into these huge shouting matches about how much we'd been screwed over by whatever. 'Cause all of us felt like we'd been screwed by someone, you know? It was hilarious. Everyone trying to yell louder than anyone else about their crappy lives." He releases a soft stream of laughter.

"But it was good. She baked cookies. Every freaking night. Chocolate chip, peanut butter, this gourmet stuff I ain't never seen before. She'd gone to pastry chef school when she was younger, but she went back to the res to take care of her dad when he was dying and she never got back out after that. She made us help with the cookies. It was fun. She was all, 'Stir, stir, *more stirring*, make the butter smooth, you shouldn't be able to feel the sugar crystals anymore.' I thought my arms were gonna fall off sometimes. But they were damn good cookies."

I reach for his hair and run my fingers through it. See in my peripheral vision how his eyes flicker to my face. "I'll make you cookies."

"That'd be good. I'll help. She taught me how to help."

The room is warm and so's the bed, and I rub my eyes with my thumbs, gouging the sleep away.

"So that's it? A couple weeks a year of good things?"

"No, there was . . ."

"There was what?"

I wait, but he doesn't say anything. Not for a long time.

WILL

I SHOULDN'T HAVE BROUGHT IT UP AT ALL. SHOULD'VE kept my damn mouth shut. She wants to know about good things, and once upon a time I had a good thing to talk about. Before I messed it up.

"Never mind."

"Tell me. I want to know everything."

"You don't wanna know this."

"Will."

She thinks she wants to know, but she don't wanna know, not really. Not her, with the way she loves little kids and doing good and all that. It's the sort of thing that'll turn her off me. The sort of thing that'll make her wonder why the hell she thinks she loves me in the first place.

Might as well know now if she can handle it.

"All right. Remember I told you about the baseball bat? After they got me outta there, I went to this new family. The Tuckers. Husband and wife, like in their forties. Real nice people. Real Christian, but the okay kind. Went to church every Sunday, and that was weird at first, but I got used to it. Didn't believe none of it, but it was all right." I stop, let that sink in. Stall for time. I shouldn't be telling her this shit. I gotta forget it ever happened.

No. I can't forget.

"Actually, I believed one part of it. That there's saints. 'Cause Mrs. Tucker was one of them. She took in the worst of us. Kids like me who got in trouble. Addicted babies. Oh my God, those babies cried all night long. But you go in there and she's just rocking them in the rocking chair, her eyes closed like she's asleep even though she got the kid scream- ing in her ear. They screamed like that all the time. All the time. They didn't wanna be touched. They didn't wanna be fed. And she was peaceful through all that like I don't know how."

Why am I telling her this? Why's she looking at me like she wants to know? She don't wanna know this. But my mouth keeps moving, like I ain't master of it no more.

"I lived with them for a year, almost. Ate a lot of weird

casseroles, but that was all right. Mr. Tucker always wanted me to call him Tom, like we could be buds. And we were, kinda. He did computer stuff from home, showed me how to take apart a tower and put it back together again. Tried to teach me computer languages but gave up on that pretty quick. Nerdy kind of guy, but cool. I thought . . . I thought maybe, for once, life had something good waiting for me, you know?"

I feel her fingers tracing the outside of my ear. It puts me in a trance and I can't stop talking.

"Anyway, it was a Saturday in October and Tom had gone and filled the minivan with wood for the stove. It was stacked all over in the car, in the way of the windows, everything. He'd parked it in the driveway, 'cause he had to unload it to the side of the house. I was gonna help him with that, but then he got an emergency call from a guy he worked for, so we had to do it later. It was nice out, so Toby, this other kid that was with us—he was almost the same age as me—said we should move the van and throw a tennis ball against the garage door. Butts Up, ever heard of it?"

I wait to see Zoe shake her head before going on. Anything to stall.

"There was another kid there, too." I swallow. His name gets stuck in my throat, so I force it out. "Ben . . . little Ben. He was two. He was a meth baby, but by the time he got the Tuckers, he was doing real good. The courts had finally signed him off for adoption. His mom had gotten into too much trouble, so they took him away for good. The Tuckers were doing all the paperwork and visits and all that so they could keep him. Adopt him, you know? Not every kid ends up in the system forever. I was a little jealous. Maybe a lot jealous. I mean, I never got signed off 'cause they couldn't never find my mom. Not that I'd wanna keep most of the families I lived with. Or that any of them would wanna keep a teenager. All they wanted were babies. That's all right. But, still."

It's dark, but I close my eyes anyway. I gotta have a darker black than this.

"So here's this Ben, cute kid, running around everywhere and got these two messed-up jerks to look up to. He wants to play with us, but I don't want him around right then. He couldn't play the game, you know? And I didn't feel all big brother. I told him to piss off. He took it kinda hard, probably didn't know what I was saying, but he figured it out. He ran off. I thought he was in the house."

I clench at Zoe's shoulders. I need something to hold on to. She's gotta feel some of this pain with me if she wants to understand me. I thought Ben was in the house.

"I get in the van, put it in neutral. Toby gives a push backward, and all that weight from the wood just pulls the car out of the driveway. And there's a bump."

"No," she chokes. "Don't tell me anymore."

"You wanted to know. You can hear it."

"Please don't."

"He was there. Ben. Right behind the car. I thought he was in the house. He weren't. He ran to hide behind the van when I was shitty to him." Zoe tries to squirm away from me, but I hold on tight. She's gotta come with me through this thing. "I didn't kill him. He's not dead. But his legs. The tires went right over them."

I feel a slow growth of dull pain in my own legs, as though the van were going over my legs, but from the inside out.

"Crushed his legs . . . I crushed his little legs." My legs shudder. "He can't walk no more . . . 'cause of me."

I'm still gripping her and I know she wants out so bad. "You want to talk about a fucked-up life? How about a kid born on drugs, then when things are about to get good, some bastard"—I make a noise 'cause there ain't a word bad enough—"runs over his legs and puts him in a wheelchair for the rest of his fucking life."

"You didn't mean to." She can barely get the words out, and I can barely hear them. Her face is buried in me, like she could hide from me in me.

"That's what the Tuckers said. Mrs. Tucker held Ben until the ambulance got there. Ben screamed. And she held him, just like she held all those babies." I loosen my grip on Zoe's shaking shoulder. "And she said it was an accident. But she cried . . . she couldn't help it. And I never seen her cry before.

Not when those babies screamed for two days straight and she could hardly stand up, nothing. I made her cry and I ruined Ben. 'Cause I was dumb and selfish. He was two. And just about to get a good life. Bad stuff happens around me. Bad stuff happens because of me."

"That's not the way it is."

"Listen to me, Zoe. I can ruin a good thing. I should've checked where he was. Hell, I shouldn't have been in the damn van in the first place. I was thirteen. I didn't know what the hell I was doing."

"You didn't mean to," she repeats. "It was so long ago."

ZOE

I MADE HIM TELL ME, SO I GUESS I DESERVE THIS HEAVY, molten blackness in my belly.

But he doesn't deserve to feel the way he is now, the way he felt all those years ago. Not again. It's my fault for not letting him keep his memory to himself. I'm torn between knowing he needed to tell me, that he couldn't scare me away, and wishing he could suck it back inside him like a layer of dust to settle at the bottom of his lungs.

"This doesn't change things." I press into him again, this time not because I feel like I need to hide but because I want to get as close to Will as possible. Let him see that I don't want to run from him, that the thought hadn't crossed my mind.

Because it hadn't.

"Do you want to tell me anything else?"

He makes a sound of disbelief.

"That wasn't enough?"

"I mean, is there anything else you need to . . . deal with?"

"This ain't a counseling session, babe."

"Don't talk to me that way. Like you're better than me."

"Me?" His voice pitches high, then lowers again. "It ain't even like that. I never thought I was better than you. Smart as you are? I just wanna move on, you know?"

"Me too."

"You still wanna be with me? After what I told you?"

"It doesn't change anything, Will. It happened a long time ago. And it was an accident. We have to learn how to . . . I don't know . . . live. Survive these things."

"Survive. Yeah. But not just that." He sucks in a breath and blows it out, hard, as though he's casting away a demon. "Like, really live, even with it all breathing down our necks. You ready to really live?"

I nod and he leaps to his feet, pulling me up with him. "When's the last time you jumped on your bed?"

I struggle for balance, thrown off by the question, by his quick movements. It's been a long time since I jumped on a bed. I tried it once. A few months after my mom died. It was loud and he could hear it downstairs and didn't like the sound of it, and I never did it again. I can't imagine how Will can switch like that, how he can go from that story to jumping on a bed. Sometimes his quick changes, the way he goes from calm to angry, from happy to sad, sends my head spinning.

I shake my head at Will and he starts bouncing. Little hops, where his toes don't completely leave the mattress but the waves of movement force my own heels off the bed. I grasp him to keep my balance.

"The . . . guy at . . . the office . . . is going to . . . hear . . . us," I gasp in between bounces.

"Not . . . through . . . the logs!" Will yells.

I give in, just a little. Just enough that I can feel gravity protesting my calves, my butt, my breasts moving against it like illegal friction. We're not on the same bounce wavelength, and my teeth chatter as Will speeds up his bounces, building height so that his head is inches from hitting the ceiling.

"Let go!"

I need to. I need to let go and let this fun, let this childish action that never fit anyplace in my life, take me over.

I bend my knees and spring of my own volition, no longer using Will's jumps to set me in motion. Our bounces are still off; we land a quarter of a second apart and I think my ankle is going to roll under my leg as I stumble, but Will hangs on to me and we build a rhythm. I coil and I leap, launching myself toward the popcorn pieces glued overhead with a forced abandon.

I will do this. I will have these fun moments and these forward-thinking moments and this future.

We hit our stride, finally, Will going up as I'm coming down, our breath passing the same space in the blink of an eye. He's grinning every time I pass him and watching me with overly bright eyes so that I wonder how much of his elation is real and how much is forced.

We can do this. We can have these moments. It is allowed.

I don't realize I've been silent all this time, concentrating, taking short puffs of air, until the first giggle escapes me and shatters my glass box. It's a strange sound: broken and delighted and free all at the same time. And it gets bigger and louder with each leap until I'm trying to match the strength of my jumps with the strength of my joy.

I lift my knees to my chest as I jump and Will spins around completely as he jumps and we're doing the craziest things with our arms and he hits his head on the ceiling with a cracking noise but doesn't stop, just hollers "OW!" and laughs and we're flying, shaking the blood in our veins like a baby's abused rattle, and my brain starts to hurt. But I don't mind. It doesn't matter until Will collapses in a pile of heavy breathing on the bed and I crumple next to him.

We reach for each other at the same time and kiss, gasping

for air in quick spurts and still laughing because this is life. It happened to us before, terrible things, and even not-so-terrible things, but now we're going to happen to it. We're going to decide and create and play and laugh and forget how to draw air in because we're so consumed with beauty and with possibility with each other.

Will's eyes are sparkling and there's a flush of color in his cheeks. I can only imagine how pink my face must be.

This is life.

We found it.

WILL

I'M HIGH. SOARING FROM THE ENDORPHINS, SOARING
away from things I did a long time ago.

I'm hungry, too.

I kiss Zoe again 'cause, damn, she tastes so good and she's
so happy right now. But I gotta get real food.

"Let's get something to eat."

She pokes out her bottom lip, but I press it back in with a
kiss and pull her to her feet. My stomach gurgles, and whatever this room and one bed and me and her lead to, I ain't
gonna be doing it while my stomach makes sick noises like
that.

"We'll run down and get some food and come back and I'm gonna kiss you all night, 'kay?"

"Yes, please."

We walk to the Denny's, just a couple of blocks down the road. The hostess-waitress woman don't give us a second look when she seats us, and I let out a breath I didn't know I was holding in. Feels like there's always someone, something, tracking us, grabbing at us, pulling us back to places we ain't good enough to escape.

"I've never eaten out so much before," Zoe says as she opens and looks at her menu. I drum my fingers through the silence between us.

"Hey, you think we're crazy?" I scratch my ear and look around at the people in the diner. Free people. "Doing this?"

She stops reading her menu for a second and I wish I hadn't asked her that question. What if she says yes? What if she says she don't really want to be here? With me, going someplace, starting something with me. But then she shakes her head. Stops and nods.

I laugh. "It's like that?"

"Yeah. It's like that." She says it the way I say it, making fun of the way I talk. It's pretty funny. "It's crazy that we got out of there and we're in the middle of nowhere and are just sort of hoping everything will turn out okay. But it's not crazy, too. It's not crazy to be with you. It's not crazy to think we can do this. We should do something really crazy. Like run down the road naked."

"Ain't it too cold?"

"Or win the lottery."

"Yeah, that'd be nice. But you gotta play first. I'll buy you a ticket when we get to Vegas. We been lucky so far. Maybe it'll keep up. We'll win a few million, set us up for a while."

She's cute and her eyes are twinkling at me. I like the idea of our whole life being set up in one day, with one piece of paper with silver scratch circles.

"We'll travel, when we win. You ever wanted to travel? We'll go to the rain forest or on a safari. Take a cruise or something. You and me. Sound good?"

She shrugs. "Go, stay. I don't care. Long as I'm with you."

"See? You're already thinking crazy."

"I'm thinking it's time to order," she shoots back, shoving me with her shoulder and nodding at the waitress making her way to our table.

ZOE

WE ORDER, AND I WATCH HIM FOR A MINUTE. HE sips his water. Peeks out at me from under his lashes. I think about his face and how it's like a mixture of everything.

He smiles at me. "What?"

"We should go see the town where you were born."

"Why the hell would we wanna do that?" The words are sharp and they sting. But he can tell and he backtracks, tries harder. "I'm sorry."

"It's okay. I understand." I get why he, why anyone, would want to forget about the place they were born. Would want to pretend the incident of birth never happened at all.

So many times—too many times—I'd wish my birth had never happened. Like when my dad was testing the strength of the walls with the back of my head. Didn't my mom know better than to bring a child into that man's world? What was she thinking, to get pregnant and then die, leaving a little girl to the mercy of a man who had no control? It's so very, very easy to blame my mom for everything, just because she made the choice to have me.

Now, looking at Will, at the way he's rolling around my suggestion in the lobes of his brain, now I can feel grateful for my life. But this life-wanting is such a new feeling. Before Will, before I knew *escape*, life was something to be endured, passively. Now I hunger for it.

Will tucks his fingers into my hair and kisses the top of my head. He's avoiding my question, I can tell. But that's all right. We all need our own time to deal with things. Maybe it will take Will years to come to terms with being abandoned. Maybe it will take forever. I'll stay with him no matter how long it takes to prove that people don't always leave, don't always give up on you.

"Is there anyone you wanna call? From back home?" He pulls his phone from his pocket and holds it out to me. "It's prepaid. I put a whole bunch of minutes on it before we left. You can call anyone you want."

"Who would I call?"

"I don't know. Lindsay?"

My best friend, Lindsay, and I met in the girls' bathroom at school when we were twelve. I was hiding in a stall, scrubbing my hands raw with a wet paper towel, when she walked in. Humiliation drowned me with a tidal wave of red. I bit my lip, stifling sound, until I thought she'd left. But she hadn't. She'd known someone was there and held her breath, waiting for me to whimper again, then knocked on my stall door. When I didn't answer, she got on her knees on the filthy floor and crawled under, facing me with a jaw set in a determined line but eyes soft and pitying. Lindsay made the same face every time she saved something: a baby bird fallen out of its nest, a dog hit by a car, the houseplants her mom couldn't help but kill with her lack of a green thumb.

She lent me the skirt she was wearing, even though her shirt wasn't quite long enough to cover the top seam of her leggings. We went to the nurse, Lin talking incessantly in the office when I felt too mortified to say a word. That year, she became the girl in my life who knew about things a motherless girl didn't know, like periods and bras. We ate together at school and studied together in the library, but I never let her come to my house and I rarely could get my dad to let me go to hers. Sometimes I told my dad stories about after-school study groups or Brain Bowl competitions that didn't exist just to have an afternoon where we could pretend we had a friendship like the ones on TV, where the girls giggle over boys and watch movies and eat popcorn and paint their nails. Always, I scrubbed off the polish and brushed away the scent of popcorn with mint toothpaste before going home again.

"What would I say to her?"

"Did you tell her you were leaving?"

"I didn't tell anyone."

"Could be she's worried 'cause you missed school."

She'd probably wonder what he did to me this time, when most things he does I try to pretend aren't that big of a deal, at least not big enough to keep me from the one place I felt safe. I never missed school.

"Okay, I'll call her." I take the phone from Will and dial Lindsay's number. It's late enough that she would be home from drama club, the only part of the school day she liked.

It rings twice. I don't realize I'm frozen, eyes not blinking, lungs not filling, until I hear Lindsay's voice on the other end and my muscles relax.

"Thank goodness you picked up."

"Zoe?"

"Yes, it's me."

Lindsay doesn't speak for a minute, but I can hear rustling and the heavy thud of feet climbing stairs on her end.

"Lin?"

"Shh!"

Another minute passes and I hear some muffled talking. Lindsay tells someone I'm Gabe from school calling about an assignment. I have to listen, longer than I want to, to her sister, Blaire, tease Lindsay in her high-pitched voice about a boy calling. Finally, I hear a door close and Lindsay breathes into the phone again.

"Zoe," she whispers. "God, I've been worried. Where are you? Are you with Will? The police came, wanting to know if I knew where you were. They have a warrant for Will's arrest. For assault on your dad. They want to find you. What's going on?"

I stare at the wall across from me, even though Will's trying hard to catch my eye. I can't look at him yet or I'll panic over all this.

"Are they tracing your calls?"

Lindsay snorts. "I don't think so. This isn't a movie, you know. But my mom and dad got so pissed when the police came. They threatened to ground me for the rest of the school year if I didn't tell them everything. But, geez, Zoe, you didn't even tell me you were leaving."

"It was a last-minute thing. We had to get out of there. You understand?"

"Yeah, we all understand. But that doesn't mean the cops care. Did you know Will's been busted for assault before? They think he stole some money, too. They told us he was dangerous. He isn't holding you captive or anything, is he? I'll get it if he's right there and you can't say anything. If he is, just say, uh, goldfish, and I'll call the cops right now."

"Lin, stop. It's nothing like that. He's never done anything to hurt me."

"But you know about his fighting problem, right? Remember Hank Prosser? He finally got a fake tooth put in. Looks so white next to all his chew-black teeth." She lowers her voice again. "I just want you to be okay."

"Yes," I whisper. "I know. And I wanted you to know I'm okay. That's why I called. To say hi and I'm fine. We're both fine. Happy, actually. It feels amazing to be free and far from home."

"Aw, you don't miss me?"

I smile at her tone. Cops or no, I know she's glad I got out of there. Maybe a little envious, even.

"Sure I do. I'm lucky I have Will, though."

"I can't believe it's just the two of you. Have you? You know."

I try as hard as I can to stop the heat from filling my face, but it's no use. I don't know if Will heard the question through the receiver, but he knows now that something embarrassing has come up.

"No," I murmur.

"Too bad. Will's cute. But, no, that's a good thing. Hold on to your principles. Well, are you sleeping in his car or what? Do you have someplace to stay? Where are you going?"

"Mostly in the car, yes." I consider her other questions. "Lin, if I might get you in trouble, I don't want to tell you where we're going. It's not that I don't trust you—I do—but I'd feel terrible if your parents found out you were keeping something from them. This way you won't have to lie. But I wish I could tell you. And I will, once we get there and things have settled down."

"It's okay, I get it." Her voice is a little wistful, but she's trying to hide it. We both know we need whatever support we can give each other. "But do you have plans? Like, what you're going to do when you get there? How's he going to take care of you?"

Maybe it's because it's helpless me, or maybe it's just the way Lin thinks, but I bristle at her assumptions.

"We have it figured out. I'm finishing school while Will works. College, too. Then I'll work so he can go to school. We'll be fine. Will does a good job taking care of me. It'll be nice to take care of him."

Will adjusts his body and stops trying to catch my eye. Instead, he grasps the back of my neck with gentle fingers and tries to rub the tension out of it.

"I have to run. I just wanted to make sure everything's okay at home."

"Your dad? I haven't seen him. But I guess he's fine. If you could put up with everything he did, he can—"

"Lin, that's okay. I don't need to know quite that much."

"Call me again soon, 'kay?"

"I will. Next time we stop. Bye."

I set the phone on the table and lean into Will.

"My dad's brought assault charges against you. They're looking for you."

"I figured as much. Don't worry about it. They'll poke around for a few days, then let it drop."

I touch the seam on his jeans, run my finger along it.

"You sound pretty sure about that. It's not the first time they've looked for you, is it?"

"I've been around some sad excuses for human beings in my life."

I nod. I know what he means.

WILL

SHE DON'T EVEN KNOW.

And I ain't telling her, don't wanna worry her, but the police are only the beginning. If there was any other way, I'd turn around and drive her back to North Dakota, do this the right way. Slowly. Let her spend our whole lives looking at me like she knows things about me that I don't even know. Let me spend forever taking care of her. But I'll never let her go back to her dad and I'll never let the system dump her in homes like I seen. This girl ain't getting any more screwed over.

"C'mon, let's take a walk." We pay the bill, suck on some sticky red-and-white mints. Move outside to get some air. "I was thinking we'd go that way." I point behind the motel, where the trees are thick enough to hide the clouds and the sky and everything else.

She gives me a look.

"What? Yeah, okay, it's a little creepy, but let's be crazy, remember? Come on."

I grab her hand and tug her into the forest. She comes with me, shaking her head, with a smile like she thinks I'm unbelievable. And that she's blaming me if she gets sick. Or eaten by a bear. But I ain't gonna let her get sick or eaten.

Not by a bear.

"Come on."

The woods are wet and smell like ranch soil after cows and rain. But better. Green. I can't figure this forest ever gets dry or dusty. Not like the Dakotas, where keeping layers of dust off your shit is a full-time job.

Zoe's hands are cold like mine, but we both warm up as we walk. She's got her coat on, and I know she can't figure how I can be warm in just my shirt. But I am. There's this blood-rushing feeling when I'm with her that keeps me heated.

Mostly the trees and stuff are so crowded that I gotta brush them aside or stomp over them so Zoe can get through. But then there's this space where something forgot to grow, or died and ain't nothing taken over yet, and the moonlight gets through to us. I stop and pull Zoe to me. We look at the stars through the hole in the trees.

"It feels like we're far away."

"From town?"

"From everything. It's just you and me and these trees. And you know what? They're gonna keep their secrets."

"What secrets?" Zoe laughs.

"How would I know? They're secrets."

"The woods make you weird."

I lower my head and catch her eyes.

"You and your name-calling."

She laughs again. Then kisses my stubble.

"Better?"

"A little."

She kisses my mouth.

"Better?"

I love this game.

"A little."

She pushes me against a tree. She's slow, deliberate. Not being her usual shy self. I like it. Anticipation churns in my chest. She runs her mouth down my neck and around my collarbone. Meets my ear with her lips.

"Now?"

I don't answer 'cause I'm too busy catching her mouth when it comes within reach of mine. She tastes like mint and smells like wildflowers pushing up through the forest floor. I bend her toward the ground, lay her on a bed of needles. Her hands are under my shirt, on my chest, and I'm sure we could sink into the ground and no one would know we were gone, would know we had ever lived. She shivers and we tangle like undergrowth.

I kiss the roundness of her ear, the sharp line of her jaw, the hollow down the side of her neck.

Her whisper: "I love you."

Sinking, falling, decomposing, the two of us into this one thing that makes the earth richer.

I kiss the skin at the base of her neck, and it's my turn.

"I love you."

Her eyes are full as she searches my face.

"Will."

I smile at her. Unbutton her shirt and bury my face in the warmth of her skin. She arches her back when I kiss that line down the middle of her stomach like I'm some kind of architect building a bridge, and balls her fists at the hem of my shirt, grasping handfuls of fabric. I let her pull it over my head and hear her sharp breath as our hot skin meets. I press my knee into the ground between her knees and feel the denim suck in water.

I want her so bad it aches. Every part of my body is tight for her.

"Will."

It's her tone—the way she says my name ain't right, somewhere in between statement and question—that makes me stop and look at her again.

The ache gets worse 'cause I know what she's gonna say.

The flush begins somewhere above her breasts and rises until it reaches the space under her eyes. She can hardly look at me, but I won't let her turn away.

"I want to wait."

"Wait?"

"Yeah. I mean, until, we, um."

She closes her eyes when I break into a grin. I can't help it. I know where she's going, we both know where she's going, and I love it.

"Until we what?"

"Until we get to Vegas. Until we . . . that is the plan, right?"

"Zoe, are you proposing to me?"

She's trying to hide, raise her hands over her face, but I got 'em pinned under mine and I ain't letting go.

"No! Wait, not that I don't . . . oh my gosh."

"That is the sweetest thing."

"Wiiiiillll."

No, I was wrong. That, her moaning my name like that. That is the sweetest thing.

"I accept."

She throws her forearm across her face and laughs.

"Will."

"I do. I mean, I will. You asked. Can't take it back now."

"Well."

"Well?"

"Well, I don't want to."

"Marry me? I guess we are kinda young."

"I don't want to take it back."

"Good."

I trail my lips back up to her neck, closing up the shirt buttons on the way. I get up and help her to her feet and tuck her into me.

"That was the plan all along, right?"

She ain't looking at me, so I can't see it, but I can hear it, the uncertainty. How do I make it go away? Ain't it enough to tell her that I ain't never wanted nothing like I want her? I squeeze her shoulders and laugh. Is it the same thing knowing that I'd never planned on letting her go, ever?

"All along."

ZOE

THIS HAPPINESS IS SO BIG, I FEAR IT WILL BURST WITH a shock of noise, like a balloon overfilled with helium. It is so encompassing that I fear it will self-destruct from an energy that can't be contained. It is so precious, I worry there will be a price to pay, a price too great, someday.

But then I tell myself that I spent the last fifteen years paying the price and that this is my reward.

We head back to the room, picking up some licorice and crackers and milk from a market on the way.

There's the one bed, so we climb in and wrap our limbs around each other and watch a little TV . . . but not really.

The volume is so low that we can only hear it when the audience laughs.

I hear Will breathe next to me. I feel his legs wrapped around mine. His arms circle my back and it's hard to breathe with my face tucked into him, but I don't mind. I feel him and nothing else, not the show, not the worry, not the freedom. Just his skin, his forearm crossed over mine, shades darker than my pale body.

"Have you loved someone else?" I ask him, not caring if he's loved every girl on earth besides me, as long as he's here with me now.

"Like, ever loved another girl?"

"Yeah."

"Not like you."

"But you've liked other girls before. What were they like?"

He dots kisses over my hair as he considers his answer.

"I'm not trying to trick you," I say. "I won't get mad."

"I've never loved anyone like I love you, Zoe. That's it. I had girlfriends, I guess, but I spent most of my time trying to survive, and the girls that I saw the most—the ones at the home—they were like sisters. And their problems were big. Too big for me."

"How were they too big?"

He shifts uncomfortably. "You've met some of them before."

I'd known the girls at the home, though not very well. At school, their hooded eyes watched me walk with Will, but they rarely tried to talk to me. I felt like I belonged to them in some ways—begging the universe for a life I wasn't fully resigned to—but in other ways, I couldn't be like them. They were brash and aggressive, forced to forge unlikely survivals. They scared me, but Will, I knew, wouldn't let them rub off on me, wouldn't let me be like them. He took me away from there, first.

"I thought my problems were big."

"Nah, you just needed to get out of there, right? But I don't know if things are better for you now, saddled with a slob like me."

I smile and nip him on the shoulder. He tastes like smooth salt, and I want to keep him on my tongue until he dissolves into my bloodstream. I let out a shriek as he grabs me and rolls me on top of him, my legs straddling his chest. He's wearing boxers and I'm wearing his T-shirt, so I feel his heat everywhere, and there's a windstorm in every region of my body as he pulls my mouth to his. He moans. I straighten my legs and blood rushes to my cheeks. I know how much he wants me.

"Let's not wait. I'll promise everything to you right now, anything you want, and we'll call it good."

His hands are places they've never been before, and it feels so good—he feels so good, his temperature, his taste—that

I'm tempted to set my fears aside and agree to whatever he says or doesn't say and does to me instead. Will is not my father.

But it's hard to let go of this thing that hovers in my belly behind the desire, this thing that confuses my body. Do I want to be touched or don't I? Frustration boils in me; I want to give in, let his touch engulf me, take me to new places— diminish my fear of new places. I want to please him, please me, embrace more than freedom of place. Break through this wall that holds me back . . . this sturdy wall. I cry instead.

I pull back and hide my eyes, but he sees and he grasps me to him.

"Okay. It's okay. You're all right and we'll wait. It'll be great, perfect, when it's time. Okay?"

I press my cheek into his chest and stare at the sliver of light coming through the center slit of the drapes. The drapes are yellow, sunshine yellow. There's a window behind them. An opening through the wall.

WILL

ZOE'S IN MY BED. AIN'T BEEN A BETTER THING TO wake up to since . . . ever. She's still sleeping, her hair's swirled all over her face and her pillow. Ain't a sound in the room 'cept breathing.

I can't stop myself from wondering what that bastard did to her. How far he took it. What more he did than plow her to the ground with his fists. Maybe that was all it took to make her afraid of everything, of me. But thinking there could've been something worse makes me wish I'd killed him when I had the chance.

Thinking she needs more to get through this than a ride

out of North Dakota scares the shit outta me.

The girls I've known, the girls at the home, the daughters, the girls walking down the street: I could tell when there was something. Some secret, horrible thing. It happens more than it should. The girls at the home talked about it like they were spilling it on some talk show.

But those girls were hard from their experiences. Zoe ain't like that. She's a soft thing lying in my bed, breathing mountain-cold morning air. I wrap a piece of her hair around my hand and move my lips to it. There's something about doing that that I ain't never felt before. Like I wanna drop the hair and move back. But I don't.

Her feet poke out from under the blanket. They dangle over the side of the bed. Her toenails are painted in chipped pink polish. Knowing these things about her, that she ain't painted her nails in a while, that she uses pink polish when she does paint them, these are the things that I wanna know. I'm desperate to know them, all the little things, as quickly as possible. Maybe when there's nothing left to hide, she won't be afraid no more.

I pull her to me. She makes a noise, smiles a little, burrows against me. I feel like we got all the time in the world to be here doing this. Ain't nobody knows we're here. Who could find us in this mountain town? Even the noon checkout time would stand still for this.

"Morning," she whispers.

"Hi."

"What time is it?"

"Does it matter?"

"Uh-uh."

"Good."

The sun comes in through the slit between the curtains and across our hips. I put my hand over the stripe, push up the sleeve of my shirt with my chin, and kiss her shoulder. The smell of her and me are mingled in that spot.

I don't care what nobody says about lacy lingerie; there ain't nothing better than this girl in my T-shirt.

"Zoe?"

"Hm."

I press my nose gently to her shoulder. "I been thinking about what you said."

"Hm?" She doesn't move.

"So, I decided I should see where I was born."

She doesn't say nothing.

"Will you come with me?"

"Are you sure?"

"About bringing you along?"

She swats at me but gets nothing but air.

"About seeing where you were born."

"Yeah. I think so. Why not? I don't care none about it, but at least you can make sure I come from an upstanding place. Probably should've done that before you proposed."

This time she attacks with her elbow, digging it in my ribs. "Ow!"

"I already know where you come from."

"And?"

"And I still put up with you. In spite of it."

"Then you're crazy."

"Okay, then. I'm crazy."

We intertwine our fingers and she pulls them to her chest. I touch my nose to hers.

"I take it back."

"Hm?"

"You're perfect."

She giggles.

"Okay, then."

ZOE

I'M NOT QUITE READY TO GET ON THE ROAD AGAIN, even if it means seeing where Will was born. The bed is warm with our bodies. The drapes over the window keep the room in a gently shadowed darkness. We lie in bed a little longer, laughing and touching. I love the way I can curl my body into him and he wraps his whole being around me and we're like this new breed of animal.

I spend endless minutes tracing his lips with my fingers and drawing my mouth across his stubbly jaw.

"You need to shave," I whisper. The tone of my voice changes the mood. Four words spoken just below his ear intensify everything. His hands tighten behind my back, pressing my belly closer to his.

He doesn't answer me except to walk his fingers under the back of his T-shirt and flatten them against my skin. The warmth of his hands spreads beyond his fingers and palm, traveling in a sunburst across my shoulder blades, my ribs, my hips. I feel him in the depths of my body. I've never been this close to somebody who loves me.

"Can I ask you something?"

His voice is husky and low in my hair.

"Of course."

"Your dad. I know he . . . pushed you around a lot. But did he ever . . . um, was that all he did? Not that hitting you's a little thing. But were there other things that he did? To you?"

I pull back. I suppose it's a natural place to go, to wonder about. But he's asking me to think about things I don't want to remember.

"No. Not like that. Sometimes, when he was in a good mood, he would grab me when I walked by and call me Debbie. It wasn't very often."

"He thought you were your mom?"

"Sometimes."

"But he never . . ."

"No."

Will brings me back to him and breathes over the top of my head.

"Does it scare you when I touch you?" A slight tremble cracks the smooth timbre of his voice.

His question is presented as self-assured, and I'm surprised when I feel the flush build in my cheeks. I know what's behind the question. I make myself catch his eyes when I answer.

"Of course not. I trust you. This is all new to me. It's too good and I don't know where to put the good. I don't want to be that way, but I can't help it. I'm sorry."

"Never be sorry. I will do anything to make you not scared anymore."

"I know." And I do know. No matter what they say about Will and about his past, no matter the anger I sometimes see in him, I know he wants to protect me, would do anything for me. It's the same way I feel, too: protective of Will, desperate to be the answer he's looking for. The girl who heals him. Maybe it's presumptuous to feel that way. But maybe it's the only way to feel.

We lie there awhile longer, not speaking, not moving, until Will rolls over and checks the alarm clock on the side table.

We reluctantly untangle ourselves, and Will goes out to double-check directions to Elko while I shower. I stand under the fierce spray of water longer than I need to because it feels so good to be clean and I know it will be a couple more days, probably, until the next shower. I'm still in the bathroom, wrapped in a skimpy white towel, when he returns. He doesn't even take the time to drop the room key but comes straight over, lifts me onto the sink counter, and covers my exposed shoulders with whisper-kisses.

"You do things to me. You don't even know."

But I do know if what he's feeling is anything like the rolling waves that are consuming me now. I grip Will with one hand and the counter with the other and take in a shaky bit of air. Then he lets go, undresses in about five seconds, and steps into the shower with a huge grin.

I feel like a trapeze artist who's had her bar and ropes taken from her midflight. Will's kiss and his beautiful naked body and the trembling in my legs are all a little too much to take. I slide off the counter and try to catch myself before I fall to the floor. I'm still unable to pull my eyes away from Will's shadow through the liner as he reaches for the soap and laughs.

"Are you laughing at me?" I squawk. I laugh, too, my voice sounds so strained. Will's laughter picks up even more.

"I can't help it. You make me happy."

I take one of the glasses on the counter and fill it with cold water from the tap. With a flick of my wrist, I toss the water over the curtain and drop the glass back onto the counter again. Will's yelp follows me as I sprint out of the bathroom and race to get my clothes on. I've managed to get my bra and jeans on when I hear the water turn off.

Will soars across the room and tackles me on the bed. He has no towel and he gleefully rubs his wet skin all over mine. He shakes his head and drops of water fly in all directions from his black hair.

"Stop it! I'm already dry!" We're laughing so hard that the springs under us squeak in helpless protest. "Get dressed," I tell him in the sternest voice I can muster, even though I love looking at him.

There are scars and his tattoo and the lines of his ribs to take in. I'm glad he's comfortable with being naked. I long to stay here and never let him put his clothes on again, just so I can look. The thought heats my chest—I want him to know how I see him, how he makes me feel. I take a hesitant breath. "I like looking at you," I say. And I try so hard to be brazen and cool when I say it, but I know I'm blushing because of the way he's smiling at me.

"And I love this way you are. All innocent and sweet."

I'm proud of the way I am but also mortified that Will has leagues more experience than I do. With life, with . . . girls. He's seen too much, done too much. And I'm jealous. I jut my chin out. "I'm not that shy."

"Yes, you are. It ain't a bad thing. I love it. You make me feel good. Important. It's not good to be like me."

"I love who you are."

He fixes me with a quiet gaze and doesn't say anything or kiss me. Just looks at me until every laugh has faded from us, then closes his eyes as though the darkness of a black hole has come upon him and he wants to welcome the vacuum like a friend.

WILL

WE CHECK OUT RIGHT BEFORE NOON AND I WALK around the car. Check the tires for tampering. Look up and down the roads. Check the rearview mirror when we leave. Nothing.

Nothing yet? Maybe just nothing and that's it. Finally got too far to be on anyone's radar no more.

It's about three and a half hours to Elko, Nevada. I don't remember nothing about the town, only that the name of it's typed on a line on my birth certificate, below the county name and above the box with my mom's name. There ain't nothing written on the line marked *father*.

The sun is low and making it hard to see, so we stop after an hour at some run-down thrift store. Next to the glass counter is a rack with sunglasses, and we try some on. They're two bucks a pop. I get a boring pair of black lenses and black frames, but Zoe, she gets this monstrous pair with rhinestones and cream-colored frames and pink lenses. She's got thick, dark bangs cut in a straight line across her eyebrows, and her lips make kisses at me. She looks like a movie star.

The lady behind the counter, skin tough and dark as a worn saddle, laughs at us. You can tell she's a smoker 'cause it's that laugh-cough-laugh thing smokers do. She waves at us and laughs again after we pay and leave.

"Thank you for my glasses," Zoe says, flipping the visor down and checking herself out in the mirror.

"They look good on you. Definitely the hottest person to ever wear them."

We get back on the highway, and the hazy sun ain't bothering us as much no more. Zoe practically presses her nose against the window to watch the scenery go by. We drove past the Great Salt Lake a while ago and she was pretty bummed with how ugly it was and the gray shore and lake. But there ain't much better to look at in Nevada. Shrub and bush and more shrub, some mountain a little way off.

Then she's got bored of the scenery and wants to look at me instead.

"You're the best-looking thing I've seen," she says, tucking her fingers in mine.

It's a great compliment and I gotta grin 'cause of that and 'cause her cheeks turn pink.

"Can't say something nice without blushing?" I tease. "You ain't gotta problem calling me names." She swats at me playfully. "I love you. Name-calling and all."

"I love you," she tells me.

I think about how much we've said that since we left. A lot. I like it. Being loved is this crazy new thing. I can't get enough of it.

She settles her head on my arm and I turn my attention to the road and to the town that waits for us to drop in like a bomb. I'm not sure what I'm gonna find there, what I'm supposed to find. I don't even know why Zoe thinks it's so important to go. What for? Find my roots, discover myself? I don't even know what the hell that's supposed to mean. I am who I am. I'm what a whole bunch of years of crap plus this little bit of Zoe has made me.

Just gotta close the door on the place. See what's left and move on. My mom ain't gonna be left. I ain't got no idea whatever happened to her. My grandma never spoke about her once. Not once. The closest I figure she ever got to talking about my mom was when she looked at me across the dinner table, that pitying look on her face, like she was sorry she ever began my line by having a daughter in the first place.

And my dad? Shit, there's a reason I got a blank spot on my birth certificate. If there's anything to learn about him in Elko, or anywhere else, it's that I don't want to be nothing like him. I ain't really sure what it means to be a man, but it sure as hell ain't what he thinks it is. Whoever he is.

Zoe nods off next to me, and she's still sleeping when we pass the "Welcome to Elko" sign, but she don't miss much. The town's about what I figured it would be: brown and low buildings, golf course of green, and housing developments off the freeway. It's just us and a couple of eighteen wheelers on the road. I turn off when I see some businesses to the right. Zoe wakes up then and glares at me through her rose-colored glasses 'cause I didn't wake her sooner.

"What? There ain't nothing to see."

We run through a grocery store, pick up some sandwiches and chips, and I ask the guy at the checkout if he's got a phone book. I flip through the names, figuring Misty ain't gonna be listed. It's been a long time since I got dumped on her doorstep. She's probably moved away by now. And Mary Torres ain't gonna be in here. I almost check, just to see if she's back for some reason. Could I face her if she was? I don't flip to the Ts, just find Mrs. Fletcher, Misty's mom, and let that be enough. I point to the address and ask the guy how to get there. He mutters about how close it is but draws a map on the back of our receipt anyway, like we're idiots.

We head back to the car.

I sit in the driver's seat longer than I need to.

"Are you okay?" Zoe asks.

I don't remember the house, what Mrs. Fletcher looks like. Don't matter. I guess she'll look pretty different after fourteen years, even if I could remember.

"All right. Ready to see where I was born?" Zoe pops open the bag of chips and crunches one. I figure that's a yes. We head into a busier part of town. I got this weird feeling that if I look up at the right moment, I'm gonna see a woman with my eyes and my hair standing on the side of the road, waiting for me to come home. But the only person on the sidewalk is a short man in black cowboy boots.

Zoe points out directions and I drive where she says, but it's stupid. I can't get myself to tell her I don't remember none of this, and even if I did, I don't wanna go backward. Last night screwed with her head and now she wants me to have some good memory come alive, or something, so I don't feel so bad no more. I knew I shouldn't have told her about what I did to Ben.

"We should just get out of here," I tell her as we go back over the highway. "There ain't nothing here."

She ignores me. I'm figuring out how stubborn she can be.

I kinda like it.

The house is yellow, a real pretty kind with white trim. None of it looks familiar: the white fence, the rosebushes, the door with the square window. What I really wanna know, though, is which of the two houses on either side used to be my mom's. Blue or white? Squat rambler or adobe? I pick the Spanish-looking one on a hunch and race to catch up to Zoe. She's already rung the doorbell.

"I don't remember this place."

But the wrinkled old woman who opens the door and stands in the shadow of the screen—that face jogs a memory from pictures or dreams or something. She looks in our eyes, then when we don't say nothing, looks at our hands.

"You selling something?"

Zoe digs her elbow into my ribs, and her bony-ass arm hurts.

"No. We ain't selling nothing. We're just . . . I don't know if you remember a kid you took in a long time ago . . ." How the hell's a conversation like this supposed to start?

The woman steps closer. Her hand's on the screen handle. She wrinkles her wrinkles as she gets a good look at me.

"William Torres?" she mutters. "That you? Look at you. You're a man," she says, and pushes on the screen. "Years'll do that to a person. Come in, both of you. I have cookies. Not homemade, but you kids eat shit anyway. Get in here. Can't see you too well out there."

Zoe holds the door for me and I step into the house.

ZOE

HE LOOKS AROUND LIKE HE JUST AWOKE FROM A
deep sleep. Takes in the furniture in the living room, swallows a few times, and runs his hand through his hair. I wasn't
sure he'd remember any of this, was afraid it wouldn't do
any good to come, but now I'm glad we're here. He breathes
slowly, as though he remembers the smell in the room,
and catches my eye as the old woman grabs snacks from
the kitchen. He takes me in his arms and kisses me in the
middle of the hallway. A reassuring kind of kiss for him, I
think.

"That's sweet. This your girlfriend?" Mrs. Fletcher shoos

us into the living room and we sit side by side on the couch, her across from us on the love seat.

"This is Zoe," Will says. He opens his mouth to say more, but nothing else comes out.

"Julie. Nice to meet you. Are you from Colorado, too?"

"Colorado?" I repeat. "No, North Dakota."

"Way up there? How'd the two of you meet, then?"

"At school. Will came to my school."

Julie looks at Will to confirm my words. He nods and she waits for more story to come, but there is nothing but an awkward silence, during which the clock on the wall ticks away the seconds too loudly. I clear my throat, hoping Will will say something, but it's Julie who breaks the oppressive quiet by standing and shoving cookies in our hands.

"I remember when Misty used to babysit you. Then your momma took off and didn't come back. You were so little you probably don't remember none of it. Folks told Misty to contact your grandma, but we all remembered Alba when she lived here, and no one said anything when Misty didn't call her after all. Now look at you. So tall. And you got yourself a girl."

Will fidgets with the car keys, twisting them around his finger until he winces. I'm not sure if he's making that face at the keys or the question he asks next. "So, do you know where my mom is? Or my dad?"

Julie's look changes and she leans close to Will. "If

Mary knew who your dad was, she'd have married the guy and wouldn't have had her nervous breakdown. That's why Alba abandoned her, you know. Couldn't stand the sight of her good Catholic girl as an unmarried mom at sixteen. So she left for heaven-knows-where and Mary did her best before it got to be too much. I bet you hate her, don't you? Your mom. But I bet she thought she was doing right by you. Misty's always been a good girl with a smart head on her shoulders."

I grip Will's hand as hard as I can.

"Where'd she go? My mom."

"Don't know. She didn't leave an address. Could be dead for all we know. Mary Torres was the kind of girl to let anyone talk her into anything. It's what comes of being raised by a woman with an iron fist."

Julie tucks a mink-gray curl behind her ear. "I'm calling Misty right now. She's going to be floored to hear I have you in my living room again." She picks up a phone from a side table and begins dialing. "You used to chew on that table right there. Surprised it didn't kill you, with all the chemicals people put on furniture."

Will and I both look at the table as Julie dials and, sure enough, the edges are ratty and missing finish. Will laughs.

"Misty, you are not going to believe who I have here— well, how in fucking hell did you know that?" Julie puts her hand over the receiver and looks our way. "She guessed it right off the bat. Says she knows you just turned eighteen. She always kept track of your birthday, you know." She transfers her hand to her waist and gives us a saucy look. "Quiet, Misty. I'm old, I don't got to stop cussing. What? What's he look like? Not much like the boy we knew. Tall. He's goodlooking. He brought a girl."

Will laughs again and it sounds like he's on a carnival ride, with the riotous lift in his laughter rising right before the sound drops away completely.

"Yeah, you'd better talk to him." Julie reaches the phone across the space in between the couch and the love seat. My hand goes to take it, because I'm not sure if Will is ready, but he beats me to it.

"Hello?"

There's a scream we can all hear on the other end, then the shrill sound fades into sobs.

"Put her on speaker," Julie demands.

Will obediently presses the speaker button and we can all hear Misty struggle for breath.

"Stop crying, girl. You can't talk to the boy if you're blubbering."

Misty responds with what I think is a demand to take her off speaker, but it's hard to be sure because the words are broken and muffled.

Will looks at me, uncertainty filling his face.

"Ask her how she's been. What she's been doing," I whisper.

"Is that your girlfriend?" comes the voice on the phone, and there's a moment of the three of us just looking at each other until we all dissolve into giggles. "I'm Misty. I don't know if Will ever told you about me."

"He told me about you. You were one of his good things."

"He always was a sweet boy."

"What've you been doing?" Will offers.

"Just living. Working. I got married twelve years ago and moved to California. I have two girls now. I've never— I never told them about you. Because I didn't know if I'd ever see you again. But I want to, all the time. I get to tell them now. What are you doing in Nevada? How's your grandma?"

"She died a long time ago."

There's a moment of silent anticipation as we wait for Misty to find the right thing to say.

"I'm sorry," she finally murmurs.

"If you're saying that for me, you don't gotta bother. We're both in a better place." There's a moment of silence when we look at our laps or the clock or the wall. Misty's breath rattles in the phone.

"Will. I tried to keep you. I called three different lawyers, and each one told me the same thing: I had nothing over your grandma. It didn't matter that I'd raised you or that we were as good as family or that I loved you—no one cared because your grandma was blood. But when she came and took you, that was one of the worst days of my life. I've waited a long time to hear from you again. Where have you been? Where did you go when your grandma died?"

"My uncle's," Will says. "Then my aunt took me to North Dakota with her, but when she got married, I went to the state. Stayed with a few different families until they put me in the group home in Fargo. I kind of got in some trouble in school."

Will stops talking and studies a small spot on his jeans before going on again.

"Got kicked out of one for fighting and then another one for . . . fighting again. Then they moved me to a new home . . . but that didn't really work out, neither. The home leader told the state I'd be better off out somewhere I could work, 'cause I needed to stay outta trouble. So I got shipped out to the boonies and spent a summer and part of the school year working on a ranch." Will shrugs, as though Misty can see him. "Wasn't too bad. But some genius figured out I wasn't even enrolled in school there and they made me enroll. But that was, like, a couple months ago, and I took off right when I turned eighteen."

"And that's it?"

"They tried to get me to graduate, then hang around and do this program. Community college with housing and stuff like that. But I just wanted to get the hell outta there."

"And you came to Nevada looking for your mom?"

"No," he says. He hesitates, slowly tracing the pattern of the couch with his finger. "But . . . you know where she is?"

There's a sharp sound on the other end.

"I don't think *she* knows where she is, baby boy. But let me tell you this—and it took me a little while to figure it out—your mom knew exactly what she was doing when she left you with me. You probably think she dumped you . . . that she didn't want you." Misty takes a deep breath. "Listen careful when I say this: your mom loved you enough to put you somewhere safe. That girl was always up and down— just like your grandma. She could have been sorted out with medication, but there was no one telling her to get to the doctor. You'd see her one time and she was high as a kite. The next time she'd have hit rock bottom."

Will runs his hand through his hair. "Was she clean?"

Misty sighs, and we can hear her settling down into a chair or couch. "Not drugs, Will. It wasn't that. It was her brain. It didn't work right. She was always up when she was pregnant. Always smiling. I'd never seen her so happy for so long. Her mama—your grandma—was out of the picture and she had the house to herself and all those good hormones. . . . I thought things were going to be okay for her, even by herself. Then she had you and she sank."

Will clenches a fist and makes a sound in the back of his throat. "So I fucked her up."

Three "*Nos!*" come at Will, but it's my eye he catches to search for affirmation that he didn't destroy his mom. I touch his wrist and he blinks.

"It wasn't you," Misty says. "It happens to lots of women after they have a baby. And for her it was worse because she already had problems. She lay in bed for weeks. Couldn't get out of the house. Wouldn't answer the phone. I let myself in every day to check on you two. I know she thought about what she was going to do. She loved you. She wrote me a letter, telling me all kinds of things. I still have it. You come see me, I'll give it to you. Mom?" Julie lifts her head from where it had been resting in her hand. "Write down my address and number. Will, you better come see me as soon as you can, hear?"

"I will."

"That's good. You come. Don't forget. I want to see what you look like now. I want to see this big trouble-maker who gets into fights. And bring Zoe. You're coming, too, right, Zoe?"

"Okay."

"Good. Did you write down my info yet, Mom?"

"Shush, girl," Julie replies. "I'm getting it. You got no respect for my arthritic hands."

"You're getting old. You need to come live with me."

"I got enough of you when you were younger. I think maybe I'll try to keep Will here instead. He and his girl can take care of me."

I feel the rush of warmth to my cheeks, and Will puts his arm around me.

"We're going down to Vegas. We actually gotta go pretty soon."

Julie scrutinizes us and points her pen at me. "She even old enough for that? Hell, she's probably not supposed to be away from home. You didn't kidnap her, did you?"

"Of course not," I exclaim as Will's arm tightens around me.

"All right, all right. Here." She passes the paper to Will. "It's done, Misty. You can lay off now."

"Good. You come see me, Will and Zoe. Remember, you promised."

"We will," Will says, but there's an airy tone to his voice, like he isn't thinking about what he's saying but about something that's already been said.

WILL

WE SAY GOOD-BYE EVEN THOUGH JULIE WANTS US to stay for dinner. Zoe's better about the "no thanks" part than I am. I keep getting lost in their conversation. Julie trying to get us to hang out longer and Zoe's nice, but firm, no and Julie tries again. Finally, I'm sitting in the driver's seat of the car with my fingers on the keys and the keys in the ignition, and all I can think is, How did I get here?

"Are you all right?" Zoe asks after she buckles her seat belt.

"Me? I'm cool." I turn the keys and listen to the car growl to life. The sound brings me back to life, too. "Yeah, I'm good."

"That was a lot to take in back there. Are you sure you're okay? I can drive if you just want to . . . think for a while."

I can't figure if I'm bothered by the stuff Julie said about my mom. Do I owe her anything? Do I owe understanding or sympathy or one fucking thought at all? She dumped me. I figured I'd done the same to her, but now I wonder if I'd hang in this town for hours just to hear more about the woman I tried pretending never existed.

I flex my scarred forearm, the dapples of pale skin on darker skin stretching over the muscles. And I gotta wonder what her arms look like.

I shrug, then laugh so Zoe don't worry. "I'm fine. No, I mean it was cool to hear Misty and see Julie. They had pretty good things to say, right?" I feel stupid for asking—for needing Zoe to agree with me—but it's the only way to know I ain't kidding myself.

"Really good. Misty obviously loved—loves—you. And Julie was so funny. I want to be like her when I'm old."

"'Cept not all the cussing, right?"

"Right. Not that."

I drive back to the highway and head east. Zoe pulls out the map and reads the freeway numbers aloud. I memorize them. Something else to think about is good. Something else to roll around in my head so I don't gotta think about other stuff, like my mom, or Misty bawling over the phone, or Julie, who could tell who I was just by looking close at my face.

"Are you hungry or anything?"

"Julie made us eat almost an entire package of cookies. I'll be full for a while."

"Nice lady," I say. I watch the rearview mirror for a minute, leaving behind the woman who couldn't take care of me, along with the ones who wanted to but weren't allowed. Sometimes things are so messed up. Like, there's an official way to do things, even if it ain't the best way to do them, and no one can see outside that. No one could see how much better I'd have been with Misty and her new family. Instead, I got . . . this.

And Zoe. I got Zoe, so it's okay.

"You think . . . you think I'm messed up? Like Misty said my mom was?"

She don't say nothing for a while, just stares out her window at the dark. It makes me think, yeah, something's wrong with me. It gets me worried. It gets me pissed—that she won't say nothing, that here's one more thing to screw with me.

She turns her head and watches me drive. I don't look at her, but I can see her out of the corner of my eye.

"How can you tell? How can you tell whether your problems are from being like your folks, or whether they come from years of being treated like—"

I swallow and grip the steering wheel. She sees it, I guess, 'cause her voice changes. It goes soft.

"Nobody treated you right. Even when times were better,

they weren't what you deserved. I don't know. Maybe there's something from your mom, but maybe you're who you are because that's who you had to be to deal. What if you're reading too much into it?" She puts her hand on mine and it's warm and meant to calm me, but my stomach's eating itself from the inside out. "Maybe you're not this bad, stupid person you think you are. Actually, no, it's not a 'maybe.' You're not that person."

I wanna believe her, but my head's spinning now and I ain't sure what I'm supposed to be thinking. I've never figured anything was wrong with me—like, brain problems. I can't get a handle on it and I don't like that.

"So, is there some test or something I'm supposed to take? To find out if I'm messed up?" I shake my head. "Actually, can we just forget about it? I don't buy that just 'cause my mom was screwed up, I am, too."

"Yeah, we can drop it. And no, you don't have to be— you're not—messed up."

"Not with you keeping me in line."

ZOE

WE STOP FOR GAS AT THE EDGE OF ELKO.

"One more tank of gas for one more stretch of highway," Will says.

I get out and he does, too. He pats the car absently and looks across the hood at me. He smiles and my insides melt with relief.

"It's okay," he says, and comes around the car to lift me off the ground in a bear hug. "Know what's coming for us? Our lives. Awesome lives for us."

The store is whitewashed clapboard with faded and chipped paintings of totem poles and eagles. Will's Camaro fits well in front of it, like it's a scene from a vintage film. Inside, there's a convenience store, a gift shop, and slot machines. Will heads for one and drops a quarter in while I walk over to the counter.

"Do you have a restroom?"

The guy behind the counter glances over me with disinterested eyes and passes me a key attached to an oar. It's more conspicuous than a neon sign. I hug the oar to my chest, all three feet of the thing, then grimace and hold it away in disgust.

"Where—?"

He flicks his thumb toward the front door.

The bathroom's outside and around the corner. Will grins at me and laughs when he sees what I have to carry to the ladies'. I ignore him and anyone else who might be looking this way and breathe a sigh of relief when I turn the corner. There's not a soul on this side of the building.

My relief fades when I see the tiny vivid fleck on my underwear and try to recall whether or not I packed tampons. I honestly can't remember putting them into my bag, and humiliation settles over me like a cloak. Not again. I can't ask Will for tampons. I've never asked him for anything that personal.

I fold a length of toilet paper and line my underwear. It's a temporary solution. There's a scratched mirror above the sink, and I curse my feminine features as I wash my hands.

How long can I rub and make suds before my hands melt away down into the drain and mix with some far-off ocean?

I take an extra piece of paper towel to wrap around the handle of the oar.

Will is in the store now, trying on a knit ski cap in shades of green and brown. There are pompoms hanging from the earpieces and he waggles them at me when he sees me hand the oar off to the cashier.

I smile at him, but I can't bring myself to laugh. One of these aisles has to have what I need.

I glance at Will. He's moved farther away, to a section of the store dedicated to Native crafts. I see him poke at the feathers on a dream catcher.

Maybe it's the next aisle.

The cashier rings up a woman with a kid at her knee screaming at her to buy him a candy bar.

Here. With the aspirin and bandages and diapers. Nice. That's the company I like to be associated with. There are only two boxes to choose from, both the same brand. Regular or Super. I figure if I get the Super, I can stretch them longer. I pick up the box to check the price sticker.

I drop the box. Twelve dollars is breakfast and lunch. A few more gallons of gas. Almost half of what we paid for a motel room.

Even if I could bring myself to ask Will to buy me the tampons, I couldn't let him spend that much. We need every dime for important things. Food. Gas to get us all the way to Vegas, all the way to freedom.

Will's in the refrigerated section, pulling out a plastic-wrapped sandwich and inspecting it.

I suck in a breath and drop to the cracked linoleum floor next to the box of tampons, ripping the top open with trembling fingers. The noise is like cascading fireworks on a windless night. I shove them everywhere, in my bra, down the back of my pants, in my socks. I don't look up. If I can't see anyone, they can't see me.

I've emptied half the box when the hands grasp my arms and jerk me to my feet.

"Stealing from me?"

He shakes my body and I freeze. Joints seize, muscles tighten, blood halts its course to my brain, fingers, ankles. He shakes me again, as though the movement will loosen my tongue and I will answer him.

He's little, dark eyes and sharp smell drifting under my nose. It's him. He's here, he's found me. I do what I always do. There's this room, four walls painted pale sunshine but no windows. That's where I hide. I'm stiff as a canoe, a vessel gliding effortlessly over still water in a sunshine room.

His face is talking to me again, but there is no Zoe here to hear his words.

With another shake, my hand betrays me, slamming against a shelf. Medicine bottles rattle to the floor and my canoe springs a leak. I whimper.

He lifts my shirt to take back what I've stolen from him. More of the same. More of the same. I can never get away.

Then, Will.

He's there, creeping up behind the cashier. I close my eyes because there is no greater embarrassment than Will seeing what this man is doing to me. I want to die.

When I open them again, it's to see Will raise his hand. His fist is wrapped around an object, dark and sloshing. He brings it down with a swiftness that startles me. The sound is dense and thudding and the man and I both fall to the floor.

Will hesitates. Swears under his breath. Drops the wine bottle to the floor, where, finally, it breaks. Rivulets of purple-red seep into floor cracks, soak into the man's shirt. He's so still. I hold my breath, waiting for him to move, a sickening feeling growing in my stomach. The bittersweet smell of wine is overwhelming.

"Will. Is he—?"

"No. Look, his fingers are twitching. Get up. Come on, Zoe. We've got to get out of here."

His hand's around my arm, too, but lower on my forearm and gentler than the cashier's. He helps me to my feet and grabs an unopened box of tampons and we run.

WILL

"WHY DIDN'T YOU TELL ME YOU NEEDED THEM?"
I toss the box in her lap. That's what I'm here for, to take care
of her. It kills me that she couldn't ask me.

"I just . . . couldn't."

She's embarrassed to admit that to me. I hate myself for
getting harsh with her. Who's she ever had to ask for stuff?
No one.

"Baby, you can ask me for anything." I put my hand on
her thigh and she covers it with hers. She's shaking and I'm
seething. I'm trying damn hard to keep it under control. I
owe her that. "I've been around girls. At the home. They ain't

shy about nothing. I get it." I try to finish with a laugh, something to reassure her, but it's a strangled sound.

Shit. I figured the bottle would break. It always does in the movies. It breaks and there's this sound of shattering glass and the impact is lessened. I ain't never heard the sound that bottle in the store made. That lumpy, thick sound. I shudder.

"They cost too much."

"They didn't cost too much. You needed them."

"We don't have enough money!"

"We got enough."

"Will—"

A fire flares to life in my head and I see spots. I tear the paper bag from under the seat. Throw it at her.

"Here! We got money."

She don't move. "Where did this come from?"

"It's our future." I didn't mean to yell at her like that. All sudden.

"You could have killed him, Will," she whispers. She don't look at me. She touches the bag. I don't want her to touch it again. I want her to touch me. I squeeze the steering wheel.

"He's gonna be fine. Better than he should be, the way he grabbed you and shook you. God, I just wanted to—"

"Don't."

"No. You didn't see it. His filthy hands on you. And you were just, like, this rag he was shaking out. You *hit back*,

Zoe, understand? He had no right to touch you. *No* right."

"I was stealing."

"So what? So he calls the cops or whatever," I shout, even though I know that'd be the worst thing. No cops. Can't have no one coming after us. "But people don't just have the right to treat you like that! Don't you get it?"

I'm yelling. My voice pings off the windows, the ceiling. But if she would just stop letting people do that to her. What happens when I'm not there, I'm working and something happens? She just gonna lie down and die?

"You gotta be stronger than that. Don't let people do things to you. Fight!"

"I never learned to fight!"

"So learn! Figure it out. You ain't gotta be your mom!"

She kinda pops—this noise—and her hand's over her face and she's crying and my heart is shredding. I'm angry. 'Cause she don't fight. 'Cause I can't hold my damn tongue when it matters, 'cause I can't take back the things she's already heard.

"Shi— Zoe, I'm sorry. I didn't mean that."

"No, I *am* like my mom."

I can't drive no more. The steering wheel's too heavy in my hands. I let go.

"Will!"

She lunges for the wheel as the car swerves away from the curve in the road. We're headed for the rocky desert, nicking a shrub before she can get us back on the road again. Her body is draped over me and she's trying to steer. She's mad or frustrated or something, but I don't even notice. All I notice is her smell, her hair tickling my chin.

"Stop it, Will!"

I ain't sure if she's talking about the car or how I'm pissed at myself for being such an ass, but I figure she means the car. I put one foot on the clutch, the other on the brake. Zoe steers us to the side of the road. We've completely stopped.

She freezes, both hands still on the wheel.

"She died when I was six. Want to know how?" Her voice is hysterical and I know I gotta shush her but I wanna hear this, too. Need to know everything.

"The stairs in my house are so steep. They're like that in old houses. Steep and hard all the way down. She fell down the stairs and broke her neck. I watched her fall. My dad and I both. Him from the top, me from the bottom. I don't know how long he'd been there, but I was hiding behind a chair while they fought. And then she fell. It sounded like . . . I don't know."

She grabs her mom's chimes and shakes them. Listens hard to the sounds of steel on steel. Her eyes are glazed over like she's just taken a hit of something.

"Like nothing I'd ever heard before. I heard the thumping of her body and her limbs . . . they all hit at different times . . . one right after the other. Sometimes two thumps at the same time. Her neck broke on the way down. I heard that, too. It sounded like . . . a firecracker. A faraway firecracker. It was muffled by her thumps and her whimpers."

"Maybe you imagined it, Zoe. Hearing her neck break. That ain't normal."

She turns her head toward me, still strumming those fucking chimes. I force them out of her hands and toss them onto the backseat. They land with an ugly sound.

Zoe keeps on. "And when she got to the bottom of the stairs she threw her arms and legs out and stared into the living room, right at the front door, like she still needed to get a little farther to get all the way out. And that's where I was. She looked through me, but my dad looked right at me. And he raised his finger in the air and pointed at me." She raises her hand, just barely, like she probably don't even notice she's doing it. "But he didn't say anything. Not a word. Nothing until he called an ambulance. He said she fell, and when they asked me if I saw anything, too, I couldn't speak. He was looking at me the whole time. And breathing . . . breathing his whiskey breath like a fire-breathing dragon."

She pauses. Hunches over. Her voice drops to a whisper. "I'm like her, Will. He pointed his finger at me and made me like her."

I put my arms around her to pull her up, but she don't wanna budge. I stroke her hair instead. Something. Anything to stop feeling useless and lost.

"Remember what you said to me? About how I don't gotta be like my mom? Same thing with you. You ain't her. You're Zoe. And your dad's hundreds of miles away. You don't gotta be like that."

"It's just who I am."

"You don't gotta be," I repeat. I don't know what else to say. Sometimes people don't wanna hear what you have to tell them. She listened real good when I said what I didn't mean, but now, when it's important and true, she won't hear me.

I force her to sit up, but gently, taking her wrists and pressing her palms against my mouth. I raise her head and her shoulders and lean them against me so I can hold her close, so she can hear the beat of my heart. I breathe steady as I can, slowing the pace for her. I gotta hope she can slow down with it, catch herself, or let me catch her.

"It took a lot of guts for you to run away, you know. To jump out that window and trust me. You took a chance, a big risk. Just being here shows how strong you are, how you ain't that person. You were just trapped for a while, but you're free now."

I got no idea if she's listening to me, even if she's just hearing me. But I say it anyway 'cause I want her to know how strong she is. She is, really is.

I want her to believe it, even if she doesn't.

ZOE

HE PULLS OFF AT A REST AREA AND CUTS THE ENGINE. I'm wiping my face furiously because it's not fair to make him feel so bad over problems he didn't create. It's not his fault that I'm spineless and weak. Not his fault that I haven't figured out how to be the kind of person that stands up for herself and doesn't let everyone walk all over her.

I hear him rummaging around in the back of the car. He's laying a blanket across the backseat, arranging pillows. I swallow back the fullness in my throat and stifle a hiccup. I won't feel sorry for myself. I won't. Will's put all this effort into getting me out of that town, out of my dad's house, and he's so patient with me. Always, I see the way he loves me.

He sticks with me. Has from the very beginning. Before this, before he asked me to leave with him, I wasn't sure how long Will would be in my life. With the school year ending in a few months, I'd assumed he'd leave as soon as he could, just like everyone who didn't have the burden of family or poverty tying them down to North Dakota. I'd figured my time with him was nothing more than a sweet intermission in a life orchestrated by the never-ending cacophony of tinkling chimes and thumping bass notes.

"Come here." He beckons toward me and I lock the doors and climb into the backseat with him. He holds me so gently and completely that I risk crying again. His smell and his warmth comfort me the way home is supposed to. His symphony soothes me.

"You know all the stuff I know about my mom. So tell me about yours," he whispers.

I think for half a second it's his way of avoiding talking about the bag of money sitting in the front seat. But that's not the way Will works. I close my eyes.

The car is quiet for a long time after he speaks, as I compile what I'd like to say about her and what I'd like to forget, the anger and hate and love and pain that surround her memory filling my body. Will's arms steady me.

"She died."

He doesn't respond to that, just waits.

"I was six. She fell down the stairs and broke her neck."

I press my cheek against the window, pretend it's the hard of a polished wood floor.

"She had full lips. I can't remember if they were just like that or if it was because they were swollen all the time. I don't have her lips. I have my dad's, and it scares me to look in the mirror sometimes. I can twist my mouth the same way he does. But I can't ever make my eyes look like his. There's something missing in mine that he has."

"You say that like it's a bad thing."

His words startle me out of my memory. I find his hand, entwine my fingers with his.

"I love her so much, Will." I splay my other hand next to my cheek on the window and dream that my fingers melt through the glass, break through it like it's liquid diamonds, and reach to the sky. If I could just touch one of those dusky stars, I could touch my mom and bring her back to me, to a place she'd be safe. We would leave like we were always meant to.

I was always meant to leave. I never thought it would take so long.

I try to grasp at the sobs before they escape me, but I might as well touch the moon.

"I love her, and I hate her. I hate her so much." I'm dying to press everything through the window. I'm so trapped here, in this car, in this life, in my hatred. I need to get out and bury myself in the ground and rise again, another girl in a new body.

"I miss her. I needed her, all the time. How could she leave me when she knew how much I would need her? Didn't she know what it would do to me? How I would love her and hate her, too, and hate me and him and be so filled with hate that I can't even cry it out? I hate everything!"

I gasp, sandy air lodging in my throat.

Just a little more. Just a little push more and I can slide through and fall to the trembling desert floor and sink in. This body is sand, dug in and stepped on. I belong there. I scream, scream, scream, and the scream feels angry and good. I pound my palm against the window and choke on tears.

"How come we didn't leave? She was a mother. She was supposed to take care of me. But she didn't. She didn't every time she let him get away with it. Why didn't she leave, Will? Why can't I stop hating her?"

"Love and hate are practically the same thing."

"Is that what you believe? Like what you feel about me is close to hate? I don't hate you. Not even close." I turn away from the window to face him.

"I hate that my mom abandoned me."

He pulls my hand away from the window and holds it in silence because there are no answers. Only motions. I close my eyes against his shoulder and stop worrying about my tears soaking into his shirt. Will can hold them. He can hold them and be better for it.

But I will never be more than what I am. My dad made me what I am: a weakling, pushed around by the smallest breeze, like chimes. But she did, too. And no mom should do that to her daughter. Girls should be strong together. Strong like steel, merry like the tinkling of chimes dancing in the wind.

WILL

"I'M GOING TO WASH UP A LITTLE." SHE COVERS HER
yawn with her hand and gives me a smile. It ain't as real at the
eyes as it used to be, and she's got circles there that remind
me of things we left North Dakota to forget, but I push that
away 'cause she don't need me being pissed right now.

"Okay. I'll be at the counter."

We tried to sleep, wrapped together, for hours. Actual
sleep didn't happen much. She talked a lot. And tossed a lot.
But I stroked her hair until she fell back into her dreams. Or
her nightmares. I fill with rage, wondering if I'll ever feel
okay about letting her dad live after all. What would've been

the best thing for her? She told me not to kill him. Begged, really. But anyone who hurts my Zoe deserves hell quick as I can serve it up.

I stand in the doorway for a minute, watching her walk down the side hallway to the restrooms. I run my hand through my hair, check out her figure in her jeans and shirt. My hands fit just right in the curve above her hips. I wanna chase her down and touch her now. Tell her again that everything's gonna be okay, but instead I head to the counter and slide onto a stool. We'll get through this. We're tired. It's time to get to Vegas.

"Morning, stranger. Coffee?"

The waitress is one of them chipper people who likes mornings. I rub my hand over my face and nod. She flips a mug over and pours, then passes me a bowl of creamers. I ignore the bowl and take a drink, loving the way the liquid burns hot and bitter in my throat.

There's a couple of old-timers at the counter. Regulars, I guess, 'cause the waitress chats with them for a minute before coming back and sliding me a menu. In a corner above the counter, a flat-screen TV plays the morning news. It don't fit, that TV, shiny and black against a backdrop of wooden paneling and old people in plaid shirts with rolled-up sleeves.

I shake my head and wonder if there's anyone else in the women's bathroom. I wanna lock Zoe in there with me and hold her until she forgets anyone ever meant her harm at all.

The oldies down the counter laugh at something the waitress says. I open the menu and close it again. Places like this got pancakes and eggs and bacon, maybe good biscuits and gravy. Ask for anything else and you're gonna get a look from the waitress that says you're in the wrong place, kid.

The weather report's over and the newscasters are getting into the local news now. I fiddle with the edge of the menu and look toward the bathrooms again. I wanna see her when she walks out. I wanna make her know I'm waiting here, just for her. I wanna watch her walking toward me and smile at her so she smiles back. For real, this time. But she ain't coming yet.

The oldies are shaking their heads at their plates now. I look at the TV screen and freeze. That face—the one in the rectangle above the news guy's talking head. I know that face. That's the face of the man that grabbed Zoe last night.

My first instinct is to ask the waitress to turn it up. To ask the oldies what happened. But it's typed out across the screen and I think I'm gonna be sick.

The waitress stands in front of me with a pad of paper.

"See what you want yet?"

"No. No, I'm waiting for someone."

I mumble the words, look around the waitress at the video footage. It's black-and-white and fuzzy, but you can see what's going on. You can see a dark-haired girl, smaller and thinner than the cashier, her eyes blank. You can see a guy, coming up the aisle with something clutched in his fist. I hear the sound even though the video don't play it. It's sick. Sicker than when I heard it in person.

The oldies, the waitress. They watch the video, the oldies' forks stopped halfway to their mouths, the waitress's hand sitting on her hip.

Then they give information on the car.

I know there's more than one old-school black Camaro on the road, but suddenly I'm fumbling for my wallet and pulling out a bill and setting it back down and there's Zoe coming, I see her out of the corner of my eye. I swear and toss some money on the table and fall outta the stool. In three steps I've got Zoe by the elbow and haul her to the front door.

She protests, but I don't look at her or no one in the restaurant. I just walk. Walk to the car, open the door for Zoe, close it.

The waitress comes out and hollers from the porch.

"Hey! You forgot your wallet!"

Zoe looks at me like she don't know what the hell's going on and puts her fingers on the door handle.

"Will, your wallet."

"Get your seat belt on."

I squeeze my hands into fists and sprint to my side of the car. The waitress is coming down the first step. I catch her eye and she's waving fake black leather in the air. My heart pounds 'cause we got forty feet in between her and me and a lot can happen in forty feet. One of the old-timers comes up behind the waitress and stares over at us. He points and says something, but I ain't hanging around to hear what. I get in the car and start it and I see the waitress's face change when she sees what I'm driving.

"Will!"

"Leave it!" I shout over the spinning of the tires on loose gravel.

Zoe says something more, but I ignore her until the road opens into nothing again.

ZOE

I CROSS MY ARMS OVER MY CHEST AND GLARE AT HIM.

"Don't yell at me."

"Be quiet, Zoe."

"I won't. I won't be quiet anymore! What's wrong with you?"

"Leave it alone, Zoe!" His fingers dance along the wheel at uncontrollable speeds.

"No! Tell me what's going on!"

"Everyone else can beat you around and you take it, but you gotta choose now to be a nagging bi— pain?"

A hole opens in my chest and the air in the car is sucked through it.

I know what he was going to say.

"Fuck you, Will!"

He takes his eyes off the road long enough to see my hand just before it connects with his face. My breath is coming at me in black-hole gasps. There is shock, shock that I just hit him. Shock that he called me a name. He's never called me a name. I've never cussed at him before.

I've never hit anyone before.

The anger is overwhelming and uncontainable and it streams through my veins like poison until I have no control over my trembling limb. My eyes fill with tears and the tears spill over a face that I know is contorted with pain. There's no room for air; it feels like I've swallowed chunks of asphalt and they can't get past my throat.

We're going so fast. Flying and I'm full of this burning and this need to hurt him more and me more and do something more to make him as angry as I am. I roll down my window. Grab the bag of stolen money from the floor, money that's not ours. Will's face turns to me in slow motion. I throw the bag hard as I can, into rock and crevice and dirt. The car swerves and Will swears.

I'm immediately sorry I did it but too scared to tell him so.

He takes it well. I can't understand how he's taking it so well. His eyes are forward, his jaw clenched, his hands kneading the steering wheel. I worry that he'll hit me, and I expect it, deserve it—want it—but he's got himself under control and I'm melting on my side of the car from rage and sorrow and pity for myself.

"We need that," is all he says.

Then why does he keep going? Why doesn't he stop, why doesn't he turn around? We can find the bag, pick up any bills that fell out.

The tension hisses and sputters between us like an angry snake, but he won't look at me. Just the road. The road, and the speedometer as the needle climbs well above ninety. He's thinking, I can tell, and above everything else, I want to know what he's thinking about. I want to understand what just happened between us, what happened at the restaurant. Why he doesn't stop to get the money. But he's acting like I'm not here, so I bury my head in my arms and let go of the frustration. I scream. Then I start to cry.

His hand is in my hair, covering my head.

"Zoe."

I'm not capable of responding to him. My tears are the Missouri River during heavy snowmelt. They choke my speech and suffocate my lungs. The car slows.

"Zoe. I'm sorry. I'm so sorry, Zoe. Please. I didn't mean to say that. I'm an asshole." He pulls off the road and yanks the key from the ignition. He reaches for my face. "No one calls you names anymore. *No one.* Especially me." His eyes dart back and forth between mine. His voice is husky. "I'm sorry. I'm— Say something."

I put my hand over his, over his arm that is creating a bridge between us, and open my mouth to say something, to make some noise that would fix everything, though I don't know what. A rhythm of shuddering hiccups takes over and I shake my head.

"Zoe." He pulls me to him, but it's awkward, like he's not sure he's allowed to bring me close. "I'm sorry." There's anguish in his voice, and part of me wants it to be there, wants him to suffer, but a bigger part doesn't. And he's not alone in being wrong. I hit him.

I want to crawl into his lap, soak in the comfort of his apology, radiate my own until it's all better.

"Will. I'm sorry, too."

He moves his hand around to my shoulder and pulls me in close, just like I wanted. I'm the bad person and yet I still got what I wanted. My father understood that when I was a bad person, I couldn't have what I wanted. He knew the punishment would atone for whatever I'd done wrong. Will kisses my head, and it's a bandage on my bruised heart, but the guilt lingers.

"Ain't nothing for you to be sorry about. I deserved that."

I shake my head again.

"No. Nobody—" I clamp my mouth shut, because who am I to say the words I want to say? Who am I to say that nobody deserves to get hit? Didn't my father punish me because he needed to, because it was all my fault? "There will never be hitting between us. Ever."

"You do whatever you need to do when I step out of line. Anything. Don't let me get away with nothing, understand?"

I kiss him hard, once, twice. Throw my arms around him and nod because he expects me to, but I can't live that life again. How hard will it be to dig out of that dark place that believes people deserve to be treated like punching bags forever?

"Nobody calls you names."

I nod again. He tucks me in as close as he can. The steering wheel wedges into my side.

He kisses my tears, my nose. "I love you."

His words, his tone soothe me, and I work on slowing my breathing. Steadying my shaking limbs. The strangely free and powerful feeling from letting myself get angry and fight back scares me. I don't want to love the slap of my hand on someone else's face. I can't be that person.

"I am sorry," I insist. "No hitting. Let's make the rule now. Never, to no one we love."

"Okay."

"Forgive me?"

He makes a disbelieving sound. "There will never come a

day when I got to forgive you for keeping me in line."

I want to make him say he forgives me, I want him to understand how I can't become a monster, but I know in his own way he already has.

"We have to go back and get the money."

"We can't."

"I bet it's right off the road, Will. We can find it!"

"No. It was stolen anyway."

I don't understand why that would matter now. Now that his wallet's gone and we have nothing.

"What happened back there?"

"The menu sucked."

"No."

I sit up, away from him, and he looks at me. There is no humor in his eyes. No devilish grin on his face. But there isn't anger, either. I saw that when I showed up at school with a new bruise. No, this light in his eye is uncontrolled and wild. I've never seen it before, but I know what it is. People like me know it on instinct.

"Tell me what's going on."

WILL

IF I TELL HER SHE'LL FREAK OUT.

If I don't tell her I'll be a liar.

I pull onto the road again. Gotta get miles between us and that diner. They're silent miles. Ugly miles.

She's waiting for my answer. Waiting like she got time, and she ain't letting it go until I tell her something. I think about the right thing to do, about what a real man would do in this situation, and all I can come up with is that a real man wouldn't be in this situation. Just fucked-up failures with too short of a fuse like me.

"It was a news story. It just wasn't a good one."

Her look is so intense it's like she's touching me. But her hands are in her lap, twisting under the pressure of my mood. She don't wanna come near me until she knows what the hell's going on.

"What's that supposed to mean? Not a good one?"

I roll down the window and stick my arm out to catch the cold. The air is this mixture of sand and weeds and it used to smell like freedom but now I ain't sure what it smells like. I ain't sure of anything but Zoe and how I'll do anything for her and of this road that stretches out in front of us for miles and miles. I just don't know if the miles are long enough.

"We could go to California now. Don't stop in Vegas. Meet Misty. Or . . . you wanted to see Mexico, right? We could do that. Just keep driving. All the way to Mexico. Get tans. Blend in. Drink tequila on the beach. Really be free."

Zoe's hands stop fussing.

"What? Will . . . I don't care about Mexico. And I don't have a passport. What does Mexico have to do with anything? Will, stop the car. Stop it!"

I do like she says, 'cause for the first time I can remember, I need someone to tell me what to do. The decisions I make on my own are crap. I need Zoe to lead me now.

We stop in a pit of sandy dirt and she gets out. She's waiting for me, but if I get out, I gotta tell her the truth. I squeeze the steering wheel and remind myself to stop being a wuss.

She's staring out over the desert when I reach her. There's

a scorpion a few feet from where we're standing, but she don't notice it. I'm fascinated by the curl of its tail, the armor on its back. I feel worse-equipped for this life than an insect I could smash under my heel. I stamp my foot in its direction and it scurries under a shrub.

She reaches for me. "What happened?"

This is better. I just had to get out of the car, out from under the noise of the engine, the noise in my head. The car is silent and so is the desert and I can figure this out. I'm gonna tell Zoe everything, 'cause there ain't gonna be no secrets and we can handle anything together.

"He's dead."

She don't say nothing for a minute. I hear her swallow.

"Who?"

"The guy. The one at the store."

All I hope for is that she don't run and hide under a bush like the scorpion.

"The one you hit with the bottle?"

I don't nod or nothing, but she knows 'cause she don't ask no more questions. We stare at the slope of low bush hills in the distance.

"Just tell me. Don't make me ask how it happened—or what happened."

So I tell her what I saw on the TV in the diner. About how the guy went home in a bad mood and yelled at his wife and went to bed but never woke up. About how the brain hemorrhage grew and grew until it finally killed him. About the woman who was in the parking lot with her kid when she heard a commotion in the store and saw two teenagers run out. About how much of our profiles was caught on grainy black-and-white film. And about the make, model, and color of car the police were looking for.

But I don't tell her about how, if I don't think about what it all means as I'm telling her, I can pretend I ain't afraid.

I turn around and glare at the car, like it's all that piece of junk's fault.

Zoe ain't looking at the desert no more. Her eyes are closed tight and her arms hug her body in a knot. She never interrupted me when I was talking. Now it's like she's trying to figure out what to say, making sure they're the right things to say.

"That's why we can't go back for the money."

I make a noise.

"What are we going to do?"

"You don't gotta do nothing. You didn't do nothing. This is all me."

She turns toward me, and those arms that were holding her together wrap around me.

"Oh my God." Her voice is high-pitched. "We have to—"

"Do what, Zoe? Turn ourselves in? We can't do that. It was an accident. Know what'll happen if we turn ourselves in? You'll go back to your dad and they'll put me away for

years. I'm legal. There's no juvie for me now. And they got
me on assault, kidnapping, theft, and now . . . this. I'm done.
Is that what you want?" I grip her to me like she can erase
it all. My heart races but I take a deep breath of her scent to
slow the panic. No one's ever helped me hold on to that calm
place like she can. If we can just get out of this and get . . .
somewhere, I know she could always keep me right. "I didn't
mean to kill him."

"I know you didn't."

"But they don't! And nobody will give a shit that I didn't
mean it."

"They know your car. And—and she has your wallet.
She recognized your car, she knows who you are, and they'll
know I'm with you, and there's nothing we can do now." She
steps back from me. Her hands twist. She's trying hard to
hold on to that place that comes just before hysterical. "We
have to explain that it was an accident!"

I grab her shoulders.

"Vegas is a big city. We can get lost there. We just gotta
get there. I'll get rid of the car. Sell it. That'll give us some
money. Change my name and find a job that pays cash. I know
what to look for. I'll do whatever I can until it all blows over.
Or we can go somewhere else. California. I'll pick oranges.
We know that it was an accident, but they don't and they'll
do everything they can to make me out like a—like a . . . I
don't know what." *I* know what I am, but I can't say it. The

word burns in my throat.

It ain't what I am.

"We just gotta keep going. I'll take care of you. We're gonna be okay, promise. I promise."

"You can't promise that, Will. People have seen us. They know we're going to Vegas. We can't get lost there. No one gets lost when they've killed someone. They'll find us. They will."

Her words cut me. I've killed someone. I ended a life. This feeling that I ain't human anymore, that I'm less than a person because I took someone else's life—that I owe them part of mine now—it don't seem to care that I didn't mean to do it. That it was an accident. And the cops won't care that I didn't mean it. They're gonna be after us now even if they weren't before.

"Then we'll keep going," I choke out, desperate to soothe her and me, too. I can drive. Just keep going until we get to that place where everyone understands accidents happen and people need to be saved. "All the way to the ocean, okay?"

"We can't run forever."

"I'll take care of you. Like you take care of me."

I kiss her all over, like it can make everything better. I promise, I say, every time my lips touch her cheek or her neck or her mouth. I promise I'm gonna step up and take care of this and of you and it will be okay.

ZOE

I'M NOT PREPARED FOR THE PHONE TO RING. THE sound cuts through the heavy silence in the car like a drill pressed to my earlobe. I jump as Will checks the screen.

"I don't know the number," he says. His voice is raspy as though his throat has seized up on him, refusing to cooperate.

He extends his hand, his fingers loose around the phone. The ringer sounds again. The area code's North Dakota. What if it's the cops? I should let it go to voice mail, make whoever it is leave a message, pretend we don't exist anymore.

No.

Even when everyone pretended I didn't, when it was easier to look the other way.

I existed.

I exist.

I press the TALK button and hold the phone to my ear but don't say anything. They have to hear my breathing. It's so loud.

"Hello? Is someone there?"

I know that whispered voice. Lindsay. I swallow.

What am I supposed to say to her? How much do I tell her? How did she even get this number? My fingers shake as I consider hanging up on her.

Except, she might have news. Something about my dad, or Will, or the police.

"Hello?" I gasp out the word, cough, try again. "Hello? Lin?"

I hear her sounds, mewling sounds and fearful sounds and hiccupping sounds. She sniffs, loud enough to fill my ear completely.

"Lin? Are you okay? How did you get this number?"

"Caller ID," she sniffs. "I erased it, though. Not that it matters. Hardly."

"What do you mean?"

"Did you hear me tell my mom you were Gabe when you called, day before yesterday?"

"Yes, I heard."

"And then Blaire was there?"

"I heard her, too." She needs to hurry up. Say what she needs to say. It's too hard to focus on anything but a dead man. "Why?"

Lindsay takes a deep breath before going on. "Blaire picked up another phone. The one in my parents' room. She listened the whole time we were talking."

I don't say anything. I'm too busy trying to remember if I'd said anything that I shouldn't have. There was no mention of Vegas, no telling her which direction we were headed. Just that I was okay. Not to worry. Not to say I called.

"She wanted to get on and tease me, I know, but then she heard your voice and listened. I didn't even hear her pick up. I can't believe I didn't hear her. I was so excited to hear where you'd gone."

"But I didn't tell you anything."

"She told my mom and dad that I talked to you. And they called the police. And grounded me forever."

"I'm sorry."

"It's not your fault. I'm gonna kill Blaire, though."

"I shouldn't have called. That was stupid."

"I'm glad you called. Except the police came over to ask me a million questions and made me feel guilty. And then . . . that's not all. The FBI came, too. Afterward. Kept asking if Will was dangerous, if I thought he made you go with him, like with a weapon. I said of course not, and they kept asking where you were, but even Blaire said you didn't tell us where you were."

"The FBI?" I whisper, my thoughts flailing too much to catch hold of. The seriousness—the way Lindsay makes it out to be so grave and terrible—isn't rooting itself in my brain. The FBI is bigger, worse, than the police. They can follow us anywhere. We can't get away.

"It's my fault, Lin. I shouldn't have called and gotten you involved. And now you could get in trouble if they find out you're talking to me again."

"It's okay. I borrowed Gabe's phone. They won't know." Lin's voice halts; she clears her throat before starting up again.

"But, Zoe, I think they know where you are. Or at least where you're headed. There's footage from this store between here and Nevada. The agents made me watch it. It looked like . . . it looked like you. Kind of. And Will. They asked if I recognized the people in the video. I saw this big guy shake y— the girl. And then the other guy . . . but the quality was really bad. I told them it was too hard to tell. That wasn't you, was it? You've never been to Nevada, never tried to—" She took another breath and lowered her voice again.

"That man died, Zoe. And now they think you're going to Vegas. Now there's more charges against Will and people in suits are coming over. . . . Tell me that it's not true, that it wasn't you in that video. Are you really okay?"

I press my nose against the cold window and stare at the silhouetted shrub and rock shapes as we speed by them. There's got to be someplace out there where people who don't mean to do anything wrong can go and live and make it all right again. A place that doesn't tear them apart or hurt their friends. Happiness can't just be a myth.

"I'm okay, really. I don't know what you saw on that video." I close my eyes now, fighting the hopeless feeling that is creeping over me like clammy fingers. "I haven't seen it. But I'm okay. And Will's okay."

I know I'm rambling, but I don't want to say something that's a lie and I don't want to tell her too much because it's not her fault, not at all, and yet things—information—get away from us sometimes.

"I'm okay, Lin. Believe that. And . . . happy to be with Will. If anyone asks again, you can tell them I one hundred percent went on my own. I want to be here, I need to be here. Everything will work out just fine. I think— I won't call for a bit, but you can call here on someone else's phone, if they won't tell."

"I'll call again. In a couple of days. Or if anything else happens here, okay?"

"Okay. Talk to you soon."

I press the END CALL button and immediately begin to despise the phone, want to crush it slowly under the heel of my shoe. I don't know where else to direct my anger, my sadness. Instead, I hand the phone back to Will, gently.

"They know where we're going," I tell him.

WILL

IT GETS REAL COLD INSIDE AT HER WORDS.

"What?"

"They know we're headed for Vegas."

"Who?"

"The police. The FBI."

The FBI. I figured this would happen. I knew they'd come. I knew we couldn't run fast enough. I figured a fake ID would be enough. I'm an idiot. Nothing's enough when you're a murderer.

"How?"

I feel like if I keep asking her these stupid questions, then

I can keep the answers from reaching me all the way. Like, each sentence that comes out of her mouth stumbles over the one before so they can't get me, can't sink in. This ain't what I wanna hear. But she does answer, saying something about a sister and a video. It don't matter. All that matters is that they know where we're going. The slipping feeling of safety that I been clinging to ever since that diner is somewhere down the road behind us now. They know where we're going. They'll be waiting there—in Vegas—for us.

No. They can't have us. They can't have Zoe. They can't take her from me.

"It'll be okay." I ain't even thinking about what I'm saying, there's no meaning behind anything. She sighs, all frustrated.

"Are you even listening to me? They know where we're going. We can't go to Vegas now."

"We're in the middle of a desert. There ain't nowhere else to go."

"Anywhere. We can go anywhere that's not Vegas."

"We already got plans."

"Listen to me!"

I rub my face and try to focus on what Zoe's saying, but her words slide by me somehow. I take her hand. It's solid, full of life. "Just let me think," I tell her.

She snatches her hand from mine, upset that I won't listen to the important things she's got to say. But it ain't like that. I'm listening, I'm trying. It's like my body won't absorb the words, though. Like they're getting deflected somewhere else before they reach my ears. I need to try harder to hear her. But then the road calls and I gotta pay attention to my driving.

I killed a man. You don't get away with that.

Run, run everywhere you can run, but you ain't getting away.

"Hey Zoe, just turn the radio on. Let's listen to some music."

She pauses, and thickness fills the car. I look at her, see her eyes narrow at me. Yes, I tell her silently, yes, you can be pissed at me for saying that, for cutting you off, for bringing you here, for putting you in this situation. You can be as angry as you want, hate me more than anyone's ever hated and yell till you're hoarse. All you want. I'm so sorry. This is the best I can do right now. Just don't leave.

She breaks eye contact with me. Her hand reaches for the radio but stops for a second. She turns to me again. Takes my jaw in her hands. Squeeze it, I wanna tell her. Hurt me all you want, like I've hurt you. But she's so gentle as she brings my face toward hers, just a little. Not enough for my eyes to lose the road, but enough so that her lips can reach my ear, my cheek, the corner of my mouth.

"I love you."

She wipes at a tear that sneaks out from under her eyelash and flips on the radio. She passes station after station until she finds a song that won't rip us to shreds with darkness or bass or anything like that. Some song everyone knew the lyrics to ten years ago but have mostly forgotten now.

I slam the back of my head into my headrest and close my eyes for a second. I can feel ghost kisses where her mouth just touched mine. Whispers of Zoe chilling out on my face. I reach my hand up instinctively to scratch at my scruffy jawline, but drop it again, quickly. I won't touch them, the angel kisses she left for me when she should've been getting out of my car and leaving me forever. No one's ever stood by me this long, through so much.

I think about what she did there with my demand that she turn on the music. Was it strength or weakness that made her do it? Was she giving in to me or was she rising above me, above everything's that happened? I look across the car at her. She's humming to the music like she got no other cares in the world.

Yeah.

Above.

So very far above me.

ZOE

I'VE NEVER FELT THIS BEFORE, THIS FEELING THAT I'VE hurt someone. If I hadn't tried to take something that wasn't mine, if I hadn't run off with Will in the first place, none of this would have happened. Will wouldn't have stolen that money. I wouldn't have tried to steal anything.

I can't stop doing bad things. Ever since I was a little girl who stood and watched, who never told because her daddy said not to.

It's dark outside already. A cloudy winter kind of dark, even though it's spring. Dark enough to close my eyes and pray to the sky or anything listening. I haven't prayed since

I was little and decided God hated me, but now I ask for forgiveness and promise to make it all right. But the only answer I get when I open my eyes is the sound of the pavement and the feeling of Will's car beneath my feet and the winking of the stars in the black sky and the knowledge that they're out there, chasing us, about to find us. The knowledge that we can't run fast enough.

I can't believe it took me this long to figure out what we were really running from. The ID, the way Will always looks in the rearview mirror, little checks he doesn't realize I see. I saw them, and I didn't get it. I get it now.

This thing we're running from is huge.

Despite how tired we are, we can't slow down. I feel frozen. Thinking too much makes me want to run, and we're already running. We trade yawns and worried looks and pats on the hand to pass the time. Will checks the gas gauge and taps the steering wheel.

"What?"

"We're a little under half a tank. We'll be okay to Vegas and getting around for a couple days."

I picture Will in the knit hat from the store in Elko and want to cry because he hasn't smiled since then.

I picture Will in handcuffs and wonder if I'll ever smile again.

The landscape starts to change under the glitter of neon lights. The freeway widens and traffic picks up as we head into a valley. I sit up in my seat and wipe my face with the back of my shirt. I feel grimy, but it's not just my skin that's crawling. A part of me is excited to see Vegas, the gaudy casinos and the masses of people. But another part of me is scared to go there. A bigger population means more police. Probably an FBI office or something. And I've seen it in the movies, the way they block off the highway when a criminal is on the run.

They'll take Will from me and send me home.

A sweat breaks out on my upper lip and I wipe it away with a nervous tremor. The traffic is moving, flowing at breakneck speeds. Cars fly around us, semi trucks take up the whole of the right lane. There can't possibly be a checkpoint, police stopping cars to look for us, at this speed.

Will is staring straight ahead. I clasp his hand and squeeze.

He jumps as though I've shocked him. "I love you," he says. Automatically, as though his thoughts are as far away as possible from loving me.

"Where will we stop?"

He drags his palm across his eyebrow and looks at me.

"I don't know."

I love him so much. How did I not realize this before, the way love grows over time, over experiences?

"How long can we go on the gas we have?"

"Maybe another three or four hours?"

What will I do without him? They'll never understand what happened. They'll take him away.

"Keep driving, Will."

"Huh?"

"Just keep going. To California. To Mexico. Wherever. Anywhere you want. They know where we're going. We have no money, no family, nothing here. Just keep going until we find a place that's safe."

"We can't drive forever."

"Yes we can. You said we could. You said so. Just keep going. We'll figure this out. We just need a little bit of money to get us through. We'll find a small town. I'll distract the person at the register and you can—"

I can't finish. The fullness of my plan swirls in my head like a bad TV drama, but I can't say the words out loud. Think it, do it. But talking about it makes it real, realer than action.

"I can't let you do this."

"We have no money, no gas, and they know who we are. You don't have a choice."

"Yeah, I do. I can keep you out of this mess."

"Don't you get it? It's like what you always tried to make me understand with the money. Everything is ours. There is no your mess and my mess. It's us. Everything we do, we do as one." I swallow back fear, thick as tar. "I'm not leaving you, I'm not letting anyone take you away from me. I'm not going anywhere and neither are you. We're in this together. Every mistake. Every accident."

My words slur at the end, my hands grip his. I search the smallest movements on his face, desperate to read his expression, to know if I've made an impact on him.

"I ain't doing this to you."

"Will. You and me."

The sky blazes unnaturally. White and red and blue and neon colors dance through the windshield. We've entered Vegas and I didn't even notice when.

He kisses my fingers and shakes his head at nothing.

WILL

JUST THIS IDEA THAT SHE FEELS LIKE SHE HAS TO DO this thing makes me grit my teeth and flex the muscles in my neck until blood pounds hard inside my head. She ain't done nothing wrong. Not yet. It's stupid of me to let her do this, to get her involved at all.

But I can't see no other way.

We pass through Vegas, all those lights and casinos and the fake Statue of Liberty and the fake Eiffel Tower. The things that were supposed to be our future, our home. But now we have to find signs to California. There are so many millions of people in California that I figure, sure, we can get lost there. And if nobody knows we're headed farther west, we'll be better off.

"I'm gonna make this up to you."

"Stop."

"I will."

"I'm so in love with you. Understand?"

The way she says it—it's different this time. Love and In Love. I don't know what to think. I struggle with my breathing, and my heart races in my chest. Those words, coming from her, aimed at a person like me, are . . . incredible. A miracle.

I begin to shake my head at her, not to say no, I don't understand, but in disbelief. That anyone could feel this way about someone as worthless as me. As much of a nothing as me. I ain't got nothing to give her, nothing at all. No job, no family, I didn't even finish high school. She's smart and beautiful. She deserves all kinds of good things, and I can't figure what it is that draws her to me. But if I did know what it was, I'd bottle it up and become a freaking millionaire.

I take my eyes off the road and kiss her instead.

"First small town."

"First one. With a store or gas station."

If there was anything else we could do, anything that wouldn't put me in jail and take her away, I'd do it.

I take whichever highway leads to California, and now we've passed through Vegas and are heading to Barstow. I wonder if the dreams I have, we have, can be met in a place called Barstow. It sounds seedy or Wild West or something like that, but I'm willing to try it.

The first town's got more casinos and hotels. It's like Vegas never ends. I keep going even though she protests. I'm thinking we shouldn't be so close to Vegas. And suddenly there's this one gas station in the desert. Nothing around it. I slam the wheel to the right to make the off ramp.

I park the car at the farthest edge of the parking lot and pull the key out. The leather seat squeaks as I move, like it's warning us, Don't be stupid. Zoe fidgets next to me. We haven't slept right in the longest time. I've got a constant thump behind my eyes. But even though she's got dark circles under them, her eyes don't look tired at all. They look determined.

I choke. "I can't do this to you."

Her response is a long, lingering kiss that melts my insides and her fingers move to the door handle. "Watch for the right moment."

And then she's gone.

I watch her stride across the parking lot and pull open the door to the store. She don't look back at me. We talked about what we would do here, planned out some ways to get the bare minimum of what we need and get the hell out.

"We don't want no one to get hurt again," I'd said.

"I'll go in and ask to use the restroom." She'd gone over

the plan again. Repeating it so I knew she had it down. "I'll plug the toilet with a whole bunch of toilet paper—or paper towels if they have them—then come out and tell the cashier the restroom's out of order. He'll go clean it up." She placed her hand on the side of my face. "All we need is a minute for you to run in, get what we need, and get out. No one's going to get hurt this time, Will."

I wait in the car for my part in her plan. After a minute, I see her walk outta the store and around the far corner. I hear a door close, and seconds later she's back. My heart speeds up. This is when she gets the cashier outta the store. I get out and walk silently toward the entrance, hide behind the ice machine. It smells like burned oil here and the smell keeps my senses alert.

It's taking too long.

We don't got a plan if this don't work, and we won't get very far on the gas we got left in the car. She's gotta hurry. My pulse throbs in my chest, in my wrist, behind my eyes. My fingers are freezing cold, but there's sweat across my forehead. I wipe at it with my forearm and mutter her name under my breath.

"Where are you?"

Then I hear it.

I leap out from behind the ice machine and yank open the door to the store. She's at the counter, her face buried in her hands. I'm off balance, lost. The cashier watches her from behind his counter, but there ain't no one hurting her. Why's she crying like that?

"I really have to go," she weeps. "Can't you fix the toilet?"

"I told you, you can use the men's."

Her hands fall to her sides. The tears leave black-edged skid marks down her cheeks and her eyes are already pink and puffy. I cringe. She looks like an addict.

"That's gross!"

"Look, kid, I'm not running a rest stop here—"

I sidle up to the counter and look Zoe square in the face. It's an act. I think. I hope.

"Hey, man. It don't hurt to take a look."

The cashier glares at me real quick and looks back at Zoe.

"C'mon, princess, I'm not supposed to leave the store."

"Obviously! When's the last time you cleaned the bathroom?"

I lean in. Like I ain't got nothing to do with this. "Sandwiches in the back?"

"Yeah, refrigerated section, next to the beer." He points down an aisle and I nod my thanks before heading to the back.

I'm checking out the soggy plastic-wrapped bread on the ham and pastrami when he finally leaves the store with Zoe. I drop the sandwich on the floor and bolt for the counter. Leap it in one flying movement. I'd hoped for a button marked with the word DRAWER. That button don't exist.

I glance at the entrance. Nothing.

I slam my fist onto the keys. No luck. I'm gonna throw the whole thing on the ground. Beat the fucking money out of it. I just can't make that kind of noise. Blood pounds in my ear. This is taking too long. Longer than it *can* take. I push buttons. The damn things beep at me, but no open drawer. Shit.

I look up again. Where are they? Slam my fists into the sides of the machine. It's too noisy. There's gotta be a hammer. Something heavy. Pound this fucker into oblivion. I check the counter, the shelves beneath it. There ain't nothing.

"Damn!"

But there's packs of gum and some other crap in front of me. I grab a pack and scan the barcode on the wrapper. Eighty-nine cents. I hit the FIVE and CASH buttons. The drawer slides open. There's paper sacks and the flash of something else under the counter. I grab a bag. Stuff the cash in. There ain't a lot, not as much as I was hoping for. But it's enough to get us outta here.

He's yelling at her and Zoe's still crying. I slam the drawer. Duck down. I see the top of his head above the magazine racks against the front window. He's coming, just a couple of steps from the door. He grips the handle. I peek over the top of the counter. See Zoe through the glass of the door. She's backing into the parking lot and he's calling her names. She raises her arm and something goes sailing through the air. The keys to the bathroom. She threw them in the bushes.

He's cussing over his shoulder as he runs to the bushes. I close my eyes against the rage building in me, but I don't got time for none of this, don't got time to feel any emotion at all. I gotta be cool and fast. Get the hell out of here. She put herself on the line for me. Let this guy say these things to her. Now I gotta hold up my end of the bargain.

I whip my fingers into the shelf under the counter and wrap my fingers around cold metal. It makes sense I'd find a weapon at a lone gas station like this one. That goes in the bag, too. Then I dart out, pause, and swipe the pack of gum off the counter. I grab a pack of cookies from a rack near the door. Stuff the bag half in my pants. I hope my sweatshirt covers the bulk enough. It'll get me out of here, buy us a few minutes.

"Girl, you gotta get it together," I toss out as I leave the store. "Hey! I didn't pick a sandwich. They're soggy as shit. You might want to check on that when you get back in."

I can't believe how calm my voice is. Like it's someone else saying everything.

I wave in the direction of the bushes. The cashier pauses in his yelling to wave me off. Zoe's already in the car when I slide in, and the cashier's still looking for the key. I wonder when he'll realize what we've gone with. I hope it takes him awhile to figure it out. We need time.

ZOE

SOME OF IT WAS AN ACT AND SOME OF IT WAS AN unexpected emotional outburst I couldn't control. I can tell Will's worried about me, about how much was real and how much was put on for the robbery.

Robbery. Theft. Kidnapping. And a dead man.

What are we doing?

The car hits a plate in the road too fast and the chimes clang, but their once lilting sound makes me think more of bells tolling now.

We stop at the edge of the next town for a total of three minutes. Just long enough to put a few gallons in the tank.

Enough to get us out of here. There are more casinos here. Flashing signs, blinking colors. The promise of luck. Even a roller coaster. I can't imagine feeling as sick on a roller coaster as I do right now.

Will jumps back in the car and we're on the road again.

He keeps looking at me as he drives. His eyes are wide and his cheeks are flushed from the tension, the thrill, or maybe just from forcing himself to stay awake.

I'm so tired that I cried because I couldn't use the girls' bathroom even though I didn't need to and even though I was the one who clogged it. I'm so tired that I could cry right now just thinking about what we did and why and how we're going to live with it all.

Instead, I press my palm against the cool window glass and follow it with my forehead. The temperature soothes me, but my heart is still racing. I thought I was used to it, being yelled at, abused, cussed at. I thought nothing could bother me anymore. But I don't deserve being treated that way, and now I'm affected in ways I've never been before. Anger simmers under my weariness, my fear, but it isn't big enough to destroy me. Not anymore.

"How'd it go?" I ask Will after a while. I splay my fingers wide and peek between them at a desert landscape of moonbeams and charcoal shadows.

"How'd it go?" he repeats. I feel his hand on my hair. That delicious transfer right out of his heart, through his fingers, and into my head. Just his touch settles my trembling chin. I can't wait until we get through this place, until we make it honestly and begin to do things that we're proud of. I can't wait to love him again without this cloud over our heads.

"How much did you get?" I'm nauseous. Will pulls the bag out from under his sweatshirt and begins to pass it to me, then stops. "What?"

The paper bag crinkles as he unrolls the top with one hand and pulls out fistfuls of cash, then dumps it all in my lap. He shoves the sack under his seat, where it hits a piece of metal with a clunk. I'm curious about the sound, about what heavy thing is under Will's legs, but fascinated by the cash in my lap. My chest swells, pride fills me, as though I earned this. As though I could do it again.

"It ain't as much as it looks," Will says. "A lot of ones. But it's enough for now."

"For now," I whisper, the words dry as desert air as they cross my lips.

I organize the bills into neat piles, smoothing the crinkles out and straightening the bent corners. Will's right. There are lots more ones than anything else. Thirty-seven of them. Fourteen fives, two tens, and twelve twenties.

"Three sixty-seven. That's more than I thought there would be. I think we'll be okay for a little while. We just need to be careful."

Will jerks his chin up at the sound of my voice. He is dozing off.

"Will!"

"Sorry. I'm good."

"No, you're not. It's been too long since you've slept well. You need to sleep. Pull over."

"You ain't in any state to drive, either."

"I'm not going to drive. We need to sleep."

"We can't stay here. Gotta keep going. What we need is to get out of Nevada."

"Yeah, alive. Pull off somewhere, please."

I wince at the whine that creeps into my voice. Will doesn't seem to notice. I move close to him and put my hands on his shoulder. I want him to look at me. He does.

"Will. Pull over."

He's so tired that his eyelid flickers a little as he looks at me. His pupils are glassy and his gaze is distant. There's a road to the left, leading out to who-knows-what. But at least it's off the main highway.

"Take this road," I demand.

He listens to me and turns off onto a road that's more dust than pavement. A few miles down there's a bend in the road and we take it, feeling secure, as though that curve can hide us from every last thing that's chasing us down.

We tuck in behind a ten-foot shrub with thick leaves and climb into the backseat. Will wants me to lie next to him, but

I shake my head and sit at one end of the seat, coaxing him to settle his head in my lap.

He does, and we spend countless moments staring at each other, letting our emotions—the ones we're admitting and the ones we're trying to hide—linger in the thin air between us. I sense his love, I wonder about his fear, his worry, if he feels those things the way I do. Am I hiding mine enough? Can he guess at the uncertainty growing in me, or is it too late to feel any of this? I rest one hand on his cheek, feel the soft mixed with the solid of his skin, and tangle the other in his hair. The strands run between my fingers like a stream of water. He closes his eyes with the tiniest of smiles playing at the corners of his mouth. How much more will it take to return that smile to his face in full? I silently promise him that I'll make it happen. We'll get through this darkness, find our hope again.

I trace the lines of his jaw, press my thumb over his lips. Lips that kiss me and love me and say my name. Lips that promise me everything he could possibly promise another person.

We are full of unfulfilled promises, me and Will.

I kiss his eyelids, his eyebrows. His breath slows as I touch him, so softly, my fingers, my lips, whispers on his face. I don't take my eyes off him. For some reason, it feels like the last time I can be this selfish, I can look at him for as long as I want to.

His throat beats a steady rhythm, and I touch his neck, marveling at how consistent and quiet his heartbeat is in his sleep when he's so intense and dynamic when he's awake. I love both sides of him: the one that soothes me and the one that can scare me.

I return my finger to his lips and follow them with my own lips, taking in the taste of him, stealing his breath, drowning in him. He kisses me back in his sleep and I tremble for his reaction that is so instinctive and affectionate.

"This isn't how it was supposed to be," I whisper against his mouth. "But I'm with you, so I'll take it for now. Whatever happens, I love you. I always will. I know you can hear this, even though you're not awake. I know you'll remember it."

I place my hand on his warm chest, settling into the slow rise and fall of his breathing like the gentle swaying rhythm of a rocking chair. I lean my cheek against the back of the seat and rest my chin on my shoulder. With a lingering wish that I could make him more comfortable, that I could take every pain from him and set it free, I close my eyes.

WILL

IT'S DARK STILL WHEN I WAKE UP TWO HOURS LATER.
A real night dark. I can't believe I slept so long when we
don't got no time, but at least it's good for driving. Night
is protecting. Zoe's asleep, her head fallen forward and her
hair dangling on both sides of her face. I tuck the pieces
back behind her ear, and she moves, resting her cheek back
against the seat.

Her breath is a wistful sigh.

I sit up suddenly, take her face in my hands, and kiss her
mouth. I take the sound from her and replace it with the pas-
sion that don't never let go of me when I'm with her. I only

feel a little bit guilty waking her, but when her eyes flutter open and watch me all sleepy and sweet and her hand comes around to rest on my leg, I ain't sorry no more. I kiss her again, and her lips and face are soft, but I barely notice 'cause I want her painfully. Her hair brushes my jaw. I feel it in my stomach, my hip bones, my toes.

My body feels urgent. The chaos we've created makes me need her more. The things we been doing, the distractions, they make me forget how right we feel when it's just us. When the world ain't creeping in. This is the perfect we been aiming for.

When she wraps her arms around me and pulls close, I feel like I've got the most important thing in the world. There's an ocean current roaring and swirling inside of me, but I force my clumsy hands to be as gentle as possible. I want to love her the best I can, even though . . . 'cause of . . . the stupid things I been doing.

All I wanna do is hold her. Never speak another word 'cept to tell her how I feel about her. I tuck her into me, dragging my mouth across her cheek, to her temple, around her earlobe. I pull her hair into a ponytail, hold it tight in my hands, so I can reach the pale skin behind her ear. She moves under my touch. I breathe on the side of her neck and realize her hands are under my shirt. But it ain't even a moment like that, like I want to toss her clothes aside and get as close to her as possible. No, it's just this sweetness, the taste of her and the smell of her and everything we feel, everything we know, together.

Nothing, no one else, has ever gotten this from me, has made me feel this way—this need to have restraint. It's kind of weird and hard, but my mind having control over my body makes me proud, like it's something I want to do more.

I pull back and watch her eyes, and she looks at me like I'm a hero and, damn, I just want to look away, 'cause I know better.

"I want to . . ." she begins in a murmur that sends shivers down my arms. She tugs at my shirt, trying to show me what she can't finish saying.

"Not here."

"I don't care. Anywhere."

"I care. You're better than here. Than the back of a car."

Her lashes flutter as she winces at my words. She settles into thoughts she ain't sharing with me. But her cheeks are crimson. I didn't mean to embarrass her. Not this time.

"I mean it. You're so beautiful. You deserve better than this."

I gotta whisper the words 'cause there's this quiet over us that can't be broken. If it is, then the world's gonna know it can come in and break into our moments. We gotta be hidden here in this new world we made. Just silence keeping all the shit of the real world away. In our world I can touch her and love her until I explode with how I gotta have her looking at me that way all the time.

"What if it's the last—"

"Don't talk like that."

"We don't know if— I—"

I press my thumb against her lips, run it across her cheek-bone. The cheekbone that's looking so much better. Pink and pale and pretty. With just an edging of bruise to remind me of all the man that I gotta be for her. I'll do anything for her.

"We have to go. What about . . . maybe . . . California. Go see Misty. Maybe she can help us."

"I think— Will, she has a family. We can't drag her into this."

Her speech is just as quiet as mine, 'cause we're busy hiding from the police and the FBI and fights and fists in our steel-and-chipped-paint Camaro cave.

I wonder what Misty's kids are like. If they're happy, if they get good grades and play sports or the piano or something like that. Stuff normal kids do. Zoe's right. I can't get them involved.

"No, we're on our own, aren't we?"

Fear flashes in her eyes. I don't know how much longer she can handle this. She ain't as hard as me.

I pull away and kiss her quickly and we climb back into our seats. I start the engine and hear her sigh as we pull back onto the highway.

ZOE

THERE'S SOMETHING PERMANENT, SOMETHING CAN'T-look-back about crossing the border into California. The farther we get from Vegas, from the plans we had, the future we'd imagined, the less I feel like I recognize this road we're taking. How long can I stall our progress before hope is lost for good?

I worry I'm going to be sick.

"Will, can we stop for a second?"

"We just did . . . ," he begins, but his voice trails off when he looks at my face. "Yeah. Sure."

The headlights crossing over the road are the only

things illuminating the desert. Even the moon has gone into hiding.

I grab a few fast food napkins and a tampon and stumble in the opposite direction as Will. I know I should make noise, that it would scare scorpions and other creatures away, but my instinct fails me. Or maybe it's my instinct that's telling me to be quiet: it's dark.

When I decide that the shadow a few yards in front of me is indeed a shrub, I head right for it. I've never peed on a bush before, but there's a primal satisfaction to it. I'm a dog marking its territory. Zoe was here.

Back at the car, Will and I wash our hands with the last of the water in the water bottle. Drips of water cascade onto the dirt, sending droplets of mud up my pant leg.

It's splatters of black on dark blue, and the more I stare, the more the spots swirl together, the less I can see anything but those dirty spots on my clean jeans.

I can't get the mud off. I can't wash these jeans. Not while we're running.

I brush my hands down my legs, slowly at first, hoping to clean away the mud, then fast, faster, as the mud smears and spreads. I'm only making it worse.

I can't stop making it worse.

I press my wrists into my eyes to hold back the screams that are building up. All because of a few bits of mud. I breathe against the sobs. Dig my fists painfully into my eye sockets. Get a grip. I have to get a grip.

I force my hands to my sides, squeeze my eyes shut, and bite the inside of my mouth. Blood races through my limbs like a raging mistral. My heart flutters like chimes.

Stop, Zoe.

Will can take care of everything.

I choke back a sob.

Do I have to believe that? He wants me to be strong. What if I choose to use that strength to overcome the evil my dad put me through—by myself? Stop letting him or anyone, even Will, lead my destiny, lead me, by the reins?

"Zoe?"

I try to answer, but my mouth is full of tears and I feel ridiculous and childish.

Will he think I'm betraying him? Am I? Is it possible, anymore, to do the right thing? As though I know what that could be. Why can't being happy, being free, be the right thing? Why can't we go back to when Will and I believed we could have the right thing?

"We can't do this. We can't go on like this, running and scared and criminal." My chest heaves against him, erratic and unstable. I have to stop this sobbing. I have to be strong for us, as strong as he is. He doesn't know what's wrong with me, what he's supposed to do. My fists flail in the desert air. I stamp my feet in the rock and sand. "I don't want to do this anymore," I scream.

Will pulls me against him, and that doesn't help at all.

I scream again. Something unintelligible. I know it's a tantrum, but it feels so good.

His hands tremble against my back.

"It's not okay. It's not. But it's gonna be. I didn't know it would—you got every right to feel like I screwed up your life. But I'm gonna take care of you. I'll protect you, I promise. Nothing can happen to you now. We're almost there. It will be okay, Zoe, I promise."

I bury my face in his shirt, grip his upper arms as hard as I can.

"Will!"

"Shhh."

I breathe. Shake my head. Raise my face to his so he can see the agony I feel when I speak.

"I want to go home."

I watch his chest seize at my words, and it's a horrible sight, then a horrible sound.

"Where you are is home to me. Why can't I be that—" He chokes on the pain I've caused, the disappointment I am. I want to tell him he is home, he is the place I feel safest, but my tongue's in knots over the best way to make him believe that. Especially when I'm starting to realize that the home I want, the Will I want, is the one who doesn't have to run from things anymore.

He clears his throat. "I won't let you go home and die

like your mom. I won't let him do that to you."

"No, don't say that, not like that."

"He killed her, Zoe. He killed your mom and he'd have killed you, too. Maybe not your body, but your inside. . . . He was already killing you. I love you. More than that. I'll take care of you. Believe me. I promise."

"Stop it, Will. Stop it! Stop promising me things you can't deliver. No more promises! We can't go on like this. We can't do this, this life of running, running, always hiding from everyone. That's not a life!"

"My life is where you are." How can his voice be so calm when I can't stop yelling? "If they take you from me, I ain't got a life."

With a fistful of his shirt, I pull him close and search his face. How can I change this path when it means we'll be torn apart?

"Listen to me," I whisper. "We can fix all of this. I'll tell them I came with you, because I did. Tell them it was self-defense with my dad, because it was. You're not a bad person. We're not bad people!"

"I killed a man."

"Will." Our bodies feel like one, my legs glued to his, my stomach flattened against his, our breath intermingled. How will we survive if we are ripped from each other? How will we survive if our spirits die for what we've done? "It was an accident. They'll see that. They have to see that!"

"They ain't gonna see that, dammit! They're gonna see what they wanna see."

"Will," I choke, my resolve fading as my words echo across the desert. "We have to do the right thing."

"I ain't gonna let them take you. I ain't gonna let them take you back to your dad."

"I can handle him now. Don't you believe me? I'm stronger now."

"You are stronger. Are you strong enough? And what about me? I ain't so smart as you, so quick to figure it all out." He's a child, a boy with hair in his eyes and pleading in his mouth. "I still need you."

He presses his face and his hands into my hair and squeezes me to him, as though he could form us into one creature, as though he could form us into a rock structure, unbreakable and unremarkable, that no one would notice out here in the desert.

WILL

IT AIN'T THAT SHE'S FALTERING ON US. ON ME. I KNOW
that ain't it. Zoe loves me. She's just never known what it's
like to not be scared of something. Like, maybe she *needs* to
be scared of something, even. It's normal for her. It's her way.

I slam my hand against the steering wheel, and Zoe
jumps. She stares at me, but I shake my head at her and she
goes back to slumping against the passenger door.

I'm a fucking prick for thinking that about her.

No one should live afraid like that. We just gotta get
through this so she can feel how it is to not be scared all the
time.

I sneak a glance at her. She punishes herself for her mom's death, I know that. Anyone could see that. It's like those crazy monks who whip themselves. She's always punishing herself, thinking she deserved to be smacked around by her dad. But she was just a kid who wrongly blamed herself for the way things were, even though none of it was her fault. A girl doing what she could to get by.

I know about that. About forgetting things on purpose. But me and Zoe, the scars don't let us forget for long. Those ghosts are gonna haunt us forever.

That's why we gotta think about the future. As much as we can. I take her elbow, slide my fingers down her forearm, grasp her hand.

"How many kids you want?"

Her mouth twitches and I want to laugh like I ain't never laughed before. Live the moments while we have them, like there ain't nobody following us and we're free as wild animals.

It feels like a long time ago we talked about it, on a night after I'd asked her to escape with me. She climbed out of her window, falling into my arms. The full moon lit our quarter-mile run to my car, parked far enough away so her dad couldn't hear it.

We sat in the backseat, 'cause it was too cold outside. She laid her head on my shoulder.

"I've never felt this way before, like I could make

arrangements, look forward to something. Is this what planning for the future feels like? Like windows wide open to the wind?"

"Sure. We can do anything," I said. "Make any old plans."

We threaded our fingers together. She never held my hand unless I grabbed hers first. But she never let go first, neither.

"What kinds of things do you want to do? Where do you see yourself in ten years?"

I let out a low whistle and rubbed the stubble along my jaw. "Ten years is a long time. Gotta have a job. And a place to live. A nice one. Big-screen TV." She laughed softly. "My car, but fixed up. You. A family."

"You want a family."

"Don't everyone want one?"

"They don't always act like it."

"Yeah," I said, detaching my hand from hers. I ran my thumb over her palm. "But we ain't like those people, are we? We got shown the wrong way. We know pretty good how to do it right. Just do the opposite."

"Two little ones," she said. "I would treat them so well, love them so much. It's not fair how some people who don't deserve kids get lots of healthy ones while others who desperately want bunches can't even have one."

"Life ain't fair."

"Such a cliché." She sighed.

She breathes heavily again now. "We've talked about this before."

"I know. Tell me again."

"Two. A girl first, then a boy."

"I want nine."

"I know! Insane. You don't have to have them, that's why you want that many."

"I want that many 'cause it's a baseball team."

She sits up a little and a slow smile spreads across her face.

"That's why!" she exclaims. I laugh at her. Damn, it feels so good to laugh again. I feel all hopeful suddenly. "But you wouldn't get nine boys, probably. Not that I'd *have* nine."

"So? Girls can play baseball."

"Better believe it. But I'm still not having nine kids."

"We'll adopt. Take care of some kids who need it."

She moves closer to me and I can feel the pity growing in her and I want to put a stop to that. I look away, out the window, see the shadows of a roadrunner standing guard on a boulder.

"I'll build a big house."

"What, out of cardboard?"

"You think that's all I'm good for?"

"The way things are go—" She shakes her head, changes her mind. "You've never built a house."

"So?"

"So, yeah, that's all you're good for, then."

Please don't stop teasing me. Not ever. No matter what happens, tease me, Zoe.

"All right, then I'll invent something to make us rich and I'll pay someone else to build us a big house."

"What are you going to invent?"

I've never thought about inventing something before.

"Mind-reading devices."

She snorts, closes her eyes, presses her fingers against her temple.

"All right, tell me what I think about that idea."

"I ain't invented it yet!"

"I can tell what you're thinking."

"Oh yeah? What am I thinking?"

She opens her eyes and gives me a look I ain't never seen from her before. It's wide eyes like she can see through me and her lips barely open like she's getting ready to say the most important thing in the world. I don't care what she says, I'm agreeing with it.

"You're thinking you're really going to do it. Go after your dreams. Figure things out. Get your big house. Your kids. And, uh, a nanny."

"You're good." And she is.

"You'll do it. You're such a hard worker."

"We'll do it, babe. We will."

She smiles to herself, a little sad. She's like that for a while, not talking or nothing, but thinking. About good things, I hope. Stuff about me. About how we've got all these hours together in this car, more hours alone together than we've ever had before. It ain't never been like that, just time that we could spend doing nothing. Real time. Our life together was built during lunch breaks and walks down the hallways and every second we could squeeze out before and after school.

Sometimes, once or twice, she would tell her dad she had to stay after to tutor some kid in science. He'd get mad thinking the school was using her for free labor, but it was better than him knowing how we'd hide away, talking for hours 'cause we had these whole lives to tell each other about and we were dying to know everything.

But now I get to learn the things she wouldn't think to tell me 'cause she never realized them. Like the way her smiles fade into a land of her own making when she stops thinking about happiness and thinks about other stuff. Stuff I don't know about and a place I can't follow her to.

I touch her hand, but she's in that place now and I'm lonely in this desert.

ZOE

MY MOM. THE BIG PICTURE IS HAZY. IT'S THE DETAILS I remember best. Warm hands that smelled like lotion. Thin wisps of hair that fell in her eyes as she bent over her work. Clandestine whispers urging me to stay in my room, where I sat behind my closed door and just listened, listened, and the shadows and tears on her face when she finally opened the door to say it was okay, I could come out now.

I remember thinking I was in trouble when she sent me to my room like that. I don't think I ever figured it out that trouble wasn't the reason she wanted me to hide. Not until the day I saw her bruises staring back at me in the mirror. Then I knew.

Then I loved her more than I thought possible for protecting me and also hated her for never taking us away from him.

My mom didn't have any family. Her own parents had long given up on having children when my mom came along unexpectedly. They were old, she'd told me, and didn't live long enough to see their only grandchild.

When they died, she married the first man who promised to take care of her.

He sure did.

I look at Will. His face is a study in concentration as he grips the steering wheel, but I don't think he's focused on his driving. I can only imagine the thoughts running through his mind. He must be so afraid, so angry, so frustrated. He helped me walk away from my dad, from blame, from being like the woman who couldn't, wouldn't, survive, not even for me.

He's the first to promise to take care of me.

I flick the ceiling light on and pull the ID he gave me out of my jeans pocket, studying the face, the birthdate that makes me three years older than I really am. I think again, stupidly, about why he did this for me. Why I needed to be eighteen as we ran across state borders together. I want to tug my hair out for not seeing it, for being so caught up in the thrill of flying that I never considered what this meant for

Will, how much trouble he could get into. How could I have been so dumb, so selfish?

All this time I've been fleeing the problems in my life while Will adds more troubles to his. How can I give him what he needs when I'm bringing him down even more? How can he be mine if he can't get out of the dark place he's in? If the FBI tracks us down, decides we did things on purpose, decides we had other choices, when we didn't, Will and I will never be together again.

I pick up Will's cell phone.

"Smile for me," I demand, aiming the camera in his direction.

He startles and looks at me curiously. "What are you doing?"

"I miss your smile so much." My voice cracks. I clear my throat. "Smile for me now and I'll take your picture so I can look at it when things are tough."

"I can't think of nothing to smile about right now."

"Not even me?"

The tension in his shoulders deflates a little and he puts one hand on my knee. "Yeah, for you I think I can come up with something."

He tries.

"That. Is pitiful. Come on, Will. Pucker up. Work the camera."

His mouth twitches, but I want more. I kiss him.

"Not enough." I take on a sleazy Hollywood voice. "Baby, don't you want to smile for me? Say . . . 'Zoe makes me hot and bothered.'"

"It's true. You do."

"Yeah, but say it!"

"Zoe makes me hot and bothered."

"Ugh."

"What?"

"If I didn't know better, I wouldn't believe you."

He laughs a little and I snap his photo. "Pathetic. But it'll have to do for now."

His hand's on my cheek. "I know. I'm sorry. It'll get better. Believe me?"

I can't answer him. I look down to avoid his eyes and slip the phone into my jeans pocket. "Can we stop for a sec so I can mark a cactus?"

Another tiny laugh, but his eyes are wary, questioning. He wants to know if it's going to be like the last time we stopped. I turn away from him.

"I drank a lot of water," I mumble, "and the road's bumpy."

He doesn't sigh like I expect him to, but quietly says "okay," and pulls to the side of the road again.

He waits in the car while I get out and pick through the shrubbery. I find the only bush taller than my waist and creep behind it, pulling the phone out of my pocket. I shiver.

Dark circles of fallen tears polka-dot the ground. How can I do this to Will? Can I convince myself I'm doing it *for* him, not *to* him? What if he really does need something . . . professional? If his mom left behind the worst of her when she dumped him? What kind of man could he be with the help he needs? Would he even get it? Is it possible for two people who never really had a chance to find someone who could turn us around? What if they take him to prison? What would my Will become then?

They'll have to know it was an accident. I'll *make* them know. Make them see the Will I know, the goodness and effort and compassion that is the *real* him.

I dial Lindsay's house. It doesn't matter anymore who might be listening in or tracing my call. Lindsay picks up after the second ring.

"Zoe?"

My hand trembles and I drop the phone into the sand. I search for it, praying a scorpion or poisonous snake bites me before I can find it so I don't do this. I brush the edge with my pinkie and pick it up.

"Zoe, is that you? Will? Hello?"

She sounds so far away.

The metal of the phone melds into my hand as it warms to my temperature. I wrap my fingers around it.

"Are you okay? Where are you? What's happening?" Lindsay's pitch is higher, the words coming out faster. The panic goes straight to my heart. I should hang up. I shouldn't do this. I should let her wonder, assume, hope I'm okay. I should tell her things are fine, I just wanted to hear a familiar voice. What am I doing?

I press the phone to my ear. It's gritty and hard.

I swallow. Choke on the bile in my throat.

I'm going to puke.

Will hollers out the window, asks if everything's all right.

There's sand in my mouth. I lick my teeth.

Oh God, if I do this—

If I don't?

"Lin? We just left Vegas. We're headed to Barstow."

I hang up.

WILL

THERE'S ONE LAST TOWN OF FLASHING LIGHTS AND casinos, then we leave Nevada and drive into California. And, man, I feel like I can breathe again. So many places to get lost here. Hell, we could hole up in the desert with a tent if we had to.

The sun's coming up behind us, glaring at me in the rearview mirror. It's barely over the horizon, and the shadows of the shrubs, the hawks on the telephone poles, the car, are long and skinny.

Zoe's been quiet for a long time, and I'm trying to convince myself it's one of those comfortable silences, but I ain't so sure about that. She stares out the window as though she can't bring herself to look at me. I've done too many things wrong. I couldn't look at me, neither. I wonder if I can change this road we're on or if it's too late. It always feels too late for me.

"You getting hungry?"

She shakes her head.

"That's good. Don't look like there's much coming for a while." She don't smile at the half-assed joke. I twist the wheel in my fists. "I've done some pretty bad things. I'm sorry I ain't this amazing person for you. You deserve better."

She faces me, finally, with big eyes and a trembling chin. "You're everything," she croaks.

I have to get us out of this. Find that freedom we had the first day we left North Dakota. We can get through this. It's all I want her to believe.

"I think I've figured out who my dad was. I think he was the devil. It runs in my veins. Still think you want to be with me?" I grin at her, try to change that look on her face. But I can't even do humor right now. She looks at me all sad, sadder than before, and I know I've failed at everything. "I've learned a lot about what not to do, you know? I just have to get down the part of what I should be doing."

She nods at me. "I want you to get that part down, too."

"I know. I will."

I rub my face, dragging the back of my fist across my eyes.

They're heavy. I'm used to being tired in my muscles after working all day, but this staying up for days is dragging on me. I swear I'm seeing a wet road in front of me, even though there ain't been rain since we got to the desert.

"Take a look at the map. Pick someplace for us to stop in California, would you? We'll get you something to eat and take a nap or something."

"I'm not hungry, really," she says, but she reaches for the map book and thumbs through the pages. She ain't really looking at them, though. She takes a breath. "Will, maybe we should turn around."

I raise my eyebrows at her. Her next words spill out in a rush.

"Go back to Vegas. You're right, it's a big place. How would anyone find us there? Maybe . . . maybe we should stick to our original plan. Instead of all this . . . so confusing. We don't know where to go in California. What to do. Who will be there. What are we doing there?"

"C'mon, Zoe, you're supposed to be the steady one. What do you want me to do? We can't go back the way we came, remember? We got no one."

She sucks on her lip for a second before letting her shoulders slump. "No, we can't go back. I just . . . don't know if I want to go to California anymore."

A nagging builds up inside me, like a roach creeping along my arm, and it's tough to find the words I need.

"You don't want to go to California . . . or you don't want to go there with me?"

She fixes me with a gaze, and my head's spinning with not knowing what she wants or don't want.

"Being with you, that's all I've ever wanted."

"So let's stop right here. Build a shelter and rough it in the desert. What do you think?" She laughs at that. Finally laughs. "Okay, maybe not. We'll keep going. A little while longer. But we'll stop soon, 'kay?"

She stares at me for a while, not answering. I look at her once, twice, checking on the road in between glances. Something's going on in her head. I hate not knowing what. There's cars behind us, red and blue. A little sports car, a pickup truck. No shiny black sedan, no white car with flashing lights. There're cars in front of us, too, putting on their brake lights, and I wonder if there's an animal in the road or something. What could be big enough to stop traffic out here?

"Are you sure you want to keep going?" She's sitting up straight, eyeing the road. We get closer to the truck in front of us and it's hard to see around it. "Are you sure you want to see what's up there? Will?" And now she's close to me, and I can smell her and taste her in the air. She's sweet like ripe fruit. I lick my lips and kiss her temple.

"What?"

"You want to do the right thing?"

I let out a breath. "Yeah. Figure there's a first time for everything, right?" I attempt another grin, but Zoe ain't having it. She takes off her seat belt and scoots onto me, wrapping her arms around me and planting her lips on mine. I press the brake to the floor and ignore the honking cars behind us. They can all go to hell.

She pulls away, a centimeter away.

"I love you."

"I know."

"There's cops up there."

I pull her body harder against me.

"I saw them."

"For me?"

She shrugs, then nods. "For us."

I kiss her again, slow, like there ain't no one ahead of us and no one behind us. Then I tuck Zoe back into her seat. The truck in front of us inches forward, and I swerve the car out of the lane to see the barricade about half a mile up ahead. Police cars turned sideways with their lights flaring, orange cones, and officers directing traffic.

They weren't behind us—they were in front, all this time.

The cars crawl through the barricade.

I ain't having none of that.

"You better get your seat belt on."

ZOE

HE SLAMS ON THE GAS AND MY HEAD SLAMS INTO the headrest. My arms flail, looking for anything to hold on to. I settle on the door and Will's elbow and squeeze both.

"I got this," Will says as the Camaro growls like a rabid wolf. We leap off the highway and into the desert, mowing over short, thick shrubs with the car's fat tires. There are shouts behind us as officers scramble into their cars and take to the sand. Will floors the gas, and the speed is electrifying. The ring of the cops' sirens swirls in my ears, the wail trading time with my throbbing heartbeat.

"Will!" I scream. I spin around, my hair whipping at my

face, to see the cops closing in on us. Part of me wants them to catch up, stop this, take us somewhere safe. The other part wants us to run, run, as far away as we can. Just go forever.

What have I done?

A sharp turn to the left and I'm flung face-forward again.

Will's mouth is set in a tight line as he leans over the steering wheel and focuses on avoiding the rocks and cracks in the earth. But they're hard to see and we hit a narrow valley, the Camaro dipping down for an instant, then flinging us into the air with a shout and a sharp spinning of the tires. We land, bounce once, twice, before the car settles back into its bumpy pace.

It's all I can do to remember to breathe. But the dust-filled air chokes me and I sputter against it, desperate to inhale pure oxygen.

Will spins the wheel to the left again and my body slams into the door. My head bangs against the window and begins to ache. But we can't stop for that.

I check the side-view mirror and flinch when I see the flashing lights behind us.

Objects are closer than they appear.

"They're right there."

Will grunts and throws the wheel to the right.

My face hits his shoulder and I taste blood.

"We're not losing them!" I shout as we leap a larger shrub

and our heads thump into the top of the car simultaneously.

"How'd they know we'd be here?" he shouts back, his eyes flickering from me to the road.

My heart races. I swear, I think I'm going to have a heart attack. I pant and shudder and grab the dash.

It's a rhetorical question, thrown out into the breeze because he doesn't realize I know the answer. Because he never dreamed I could have betrayed him like this.

But I did.

"Will."

"Not a good time."

"I love you."

"Love you, too," he says distractedly.

I raise my voice to be heard over the sounds of the chase. "No, I mean. . . . . I *love* you. I thought I loved you before we left. And a couple days ago I thought that, too . . . but what I feel now is bigger. The kind of bigger that makes me want to do the right thing. You make me need to do the right thing. Our love like this, grown while we committed crimes—it's going to destroy us."

His eyebrows knit together as he tries to process what I'm saying in between steering the car around mounds and craters in the dirt. The words are rushed, falling over each other in their haste to get out of my mouth. He gives up and absently squeezes my knee before returning his hand to the wheel. I'll tell you this again later, I promise silently, when this is all over and we're together and life is better—the *real* better we planned it to be.

We're approaching jagged hills. We can't go much farther and I want to tell him that, want to tell him how sorry I am, but he's determined to get around them. We careen left, the tires skidding in the sand and the back end of the car rounding us off course. The cops are set to T-bone right into Will's side. My heart races and I can't let that happen; I can't let him get hurt.

In that instant I don't care what anyone thinks of me, as long as nothing happens to Will. I have to get us out of here. How could I have called—how could I have destroyed us like that?

My head whips toward Will as the cop car looms out of the desert at a speed that could rip Will's car in two. I shove Will's shoulder desperately.

"Go!" I scream madly. "Go!"

Will resets the wheel and presses the gas to the floor and we're off again, the first police car dinging into the rear bumper as we break.

It takes a few seconds for the cops to orient themselves to our new path, and by then Will's discovered a dirt-and-gravel road. He swerves us onto it, and I hear the engine roar with pleasure as the speedometer needle rises.

The road is still bumpy, and I clamp my teeth together to stop the chattering. It's not just the road causing the tremors.

The cops are farther behind now but shouting things at us. I hear their words echo off the rock formations. They've probably been shouting all along.

"They're going to shoot, Will."

"Tires are hard to hit."

"We can't run forever."

"You just gotta trust me."

"I do. I trust you, and I love you, and I want you."

"Okay, then."

But tires *aren't* that hard to hit, apparently. I shriek at the explosive sound of bullet hitting hot rubber, and we skid off the road. Will swears and tries to control the steering wheel, but it seems to have a mind of its own. My eyes widen at the size of the rock directly in front of us and I scream, but Will already sees it. He slams on the brake. The car locks up, but the sand can't hold us and the crash sends my face into the dash and sets my ears ringing. I rub my nose gingerly, coming away with streaks of sticky, warm blood on my knuckles.

"Zoe," Will mumbles.

There's a gash under his eye, but he wipes at it carelessly and reaches for my face and covers my mouth with a kiss that dismisses thought and pain and sorrow and everything else but him and me.

"You're everything," he breathes.

My eyes water. The tears are filled with a million molecules of hurt and regret. My face feels like it went a round with my dad, but my tears are for something else. I suck a bit of air in and let it out as an agonizing sob.

"I love you, Will."

"I know."

"Be-lieve me?"

"Yeah."

I choke on the sobs and taste the snot and blood as it flows from my nose and over my lip.

"I told." I look away from him as my voice breaks. It takes everything I have just to inhale sharp little puffs of air and let them back out again. "I— told Lin. About Barstow. I thought . . . I thought you would be better without me."

His hand drops from my hair, and that makes it worse, makes the cries come harder. He's given up on me, if he won't touch me. I would abandon me, too.

"That's how they knew where we were."

I nod and wipe my nose on the back of my sleeve and hiccup.

He breaks into that devilish smile I adore.

"Damn." He laughs. As if there's nothing left to do *but* laugh. "If I'da known we were throwing in the towel, I would've enjoyed the chase more."

WILL

THEY'RE YELLING OUTSIDE THE CAR, AND THERE AIN'T much time left.

I take her face in my hands. Probably for the last time for a long time. Maybe ever. There's guilt splashed across it and a look like she wants to die, and I stop smiling.

My Zoe.

"You did right," I tell her. "You're better than I could ever be, you know that? 'Cause you do the right thing. You're so fucking beautiful. You're an angel. And you know—" I make a grasping, chesty sound. "You know fucking everything and . . . everything, about me. And you still love me, don't you?"

She nods. Then she flings herself into my lap.

"I'm sorry," she chokes.

"You want to save me. Bad as I want to save you. I know about that."

She covers me with lips wet with tears, all over, and she's part of me, everything of me, until there ain't nothing left of Will and only this better unnamed thing that I am now, because of her.

The cops are inching toward us. The morning sun glints off their badges, their guns.

Zoe watches me with wide eyes and I smile at her. My chest explodes with the love I got for her. I press my thumb against her lips and she kisses it, sending tremors down my spine.

"Let's go," I say. She waits, follows my lead. My head is bobbing at her in this sort of auto-nod. Like it's going to be okay. Like I know they ain't gonna take her from me. Like I know they ain't gonna toss her back into that hell with her dad. Like they'll understand everything and let us go.

But this life taught me different. Nobody cares if it ain't your fault or if you didn't mean to. No one cares if you need some help—all there is is people spitting at you. It's you against the world, and when the world's bigger, what's left to do but give up?

Zoe can do better without me. She needs something better than this.

She's halfway out of the car when I reach under my seat, grasp the cold of a black metal handle in my hand, finger the trigger, fling the door open. All this in the time it takes her eyes to widen even farther.

"Will—no!"

But I'm already out of the car.

ZOE

THEY YELL WHEN THEY SEE THE GUN. NO, NOT YELL.
They scream. A sound filled with shock and fear and fury.
They scream at him to drop his weapon, that they will shoot
if they have to.

I run for Will.

WILL

I WANT HER TO STAY AWAY. I PUT MY ARM OUT TO keep her away. This was something she never should've been dragged into. But she comes anyway and I tuck her into me anyway because I can't help it. I wish it were where she belongs. Where I belong. But she's gotta get away from me.

ZOE

ONE ARM IS AROUND ME. THE OTHER EXTENDS beyond us, and I look away from it to the expanse of the desert behind us, try not to see it, pretend the arm and the curled fingers and the weapon at the end of it don't exist.

What is he doing? What is he thinking? Does he want to get himself killed?

And then I realize.

Sometimes, it's just time. Time to pay, time to reckon. I've spent my childhood hiding who killed my mother. There's no punishment big enough for me. Not my dad's fists, not years of invisibility.

I spin around. Fan my arms out. Face them. Face every-thing. Will holds me still. I want them to take me in the worst way possible. And I want him to let me fall when they do.

This happiness was never meant for me.

WILL

THEY'RE GONNA THINK I'M HOLDING HER HOSTAGE.
The way I got her. The blood under her nose, on her lips. Do
they see the way her back's pressed to me, the way her body
trembles? Or are they only seeing what they want to see?
Maybe it's me that's been blind all this time. I've gone and
hurt people in my life. Now I'm gonna get what I deserve.

ZOE

"STAY BACK!"

Will's yelling at them. As if we could stand here forever, here in the desert with these figures in uniforms and suits and more pulling up as we stand. With the desert dirt and rock and the crushed Camaro. With Will hanging on with one hand, and in the other, a gun pointing at them and their guns pointing at us.

I don't know what Will's doing, what he's thinking, what he's hoping, but I'm not afraid.

WILL

"LET THE GIRL GO!" THEY YELL, AND I HAVE THE MAD desire to laugh.

I can't. I need to, 'cause she's gonna be better off, but I can't let her go. They don't get it, how she's the only one who would've come this far with me.

ZOE

PLEASE DON'T SHOOT, WILL. PUT DOWN THE GUN.
I want to live.

WILL

"DROP YOUR WEAPON!"

I ain't never shot a gun before. I don't know if I can shoot this one.

I can't drop it. I can't let it go. I don't know what I'm doing with it, why it's here. Why can't my brain work as fast as my body?

My hand shakes.

I want to live.

ZOE

WILL'S BODY SHUDDERS. I TURN MY FACE TO HIS.

WILL

I PULL ZOE UP TO MY MOUTH AND PRESS A KISS TO her, a harder kiss than I've ever given. A kiss that burns us both. I memorize her face in the one second it takes for me to make this decision, then I push her away from me. I shove her into the dirt, toward them. I'm mean and angry, not 'cause of anything she did, but 'cause now I finally get it. It's 'cause of everything I didn't do. Of everything no one ever taught me how to do.

What it means to be a man, to love someone this much. Enough to give everything I am.

Life is meant for her. She deserves every wonderful thing.

Without me, she's gonna get it, too. All the good stuff. It's time for me to go in.

I surrender. Begin to raise my hands.

They tremble.

The gun shakes violently.

There's an explosive noise, close to my ear. My arm flings backward, farther than my shoulder should let it.

Then there're echoes all over the desert.

I stumble.

Zoe's lifting her head, so slowly, like she's emerging from ice.

There's dynamite going off in my chest. In my leg. My neck.

Tingling in my arms, ribs. The ground.

My head bounces off the dirt before it settles again.

It's slow. My legs are gone. Lungs won't open. Bugs are crawling through my blood.

But I don't mind. Zoe's right here. She's fallen next to me. I reach my hand to her face, open my mouth to whisper her name, but there's this awful taste in my mouth and a thick, warm liquid seeping in. I can't speak. I gag on my words.

Zoe's eyes lock with mine and I can't look away and it's the sweetest, sweetest thing. She'll be safe. They ain't never gonna take her back to her dad. They'll see they can't. It's the one good thing I've done in this life: kept that promise to help make her stronger. She'll know where to go from here.

I see it. In her eyes, in the set of her mouth. She won't let them do nothing bad to her.

I rest my head back against the ground. I'm so tired. All the exhilaration of the chase, of running, of standing my ground, has faded and left me damn tired.

It's dark.

I did what I had to do.

She'll live. Live wonderful.

And there ain't nothing bigger than that.

ZOE

HE FALLS INTO ME AND ONTO ME AND OVER ME AND there is blood everywhere I can taste it in the air and in my mouth just like his kisses my blood and his, too, and in my nose even though it is impossible to breathe and I can't find the air, the strength to suck it down.

"You promised me. You promised. You promised you'd take care of me. You promised you'd take me to see the ocean. Get up. Get up and take me, you promised, you *promised*. I'll take your promises now, I believed them then. I did really. Promise me *something*. Will, I'll believe you!"

The anger and the screaming are consuming and they

feel so, so good right now, when I know that feeling anything else would kill me.

The screaming is the only thing that keeps me from wanting to die, too.

"No, no, Will. *Will!* God, no!"

It's like he's letting himself go. Like he's not fighting the holes, the rivulets of blood.

I look at them. Those people.

"You fuckers!" It tastes so good to say it. "You fucking fuckers! Get away from us!"

They're coming. They're going to take Will.

I clutch him to me. He's mine. They can't have him. They don't know him, but I do. He's mine. My everything. He made me see. He believed in me and my strength. I press my palm over his stomach. Another over his neck. But I don't have enough hands and I have to stop the bleeding. I need to know how to do this, how to save lives. But I only have two hands.

I lay on top of him. Press my cheek onto his chest and feel the warm, slippery oozing against my skin. The smell is overwhelming, but I won't move. His blood gathers in the corner of my lips and seeps into my mouth. His taste is the same as mine, our blood is the same blood. I close my eyes because *they're still coming*, but I have to stop the bleeding and they need to stay back while I stop the bleeding. My ear's right there, right where I should be able to hear his life, but there's nothing. Nothing.

Nothing.

I hear nothing.

Feel nothing.

The anger is over. And the screaming. People surround me, grab me, *touch* me. Touch Will. Kneel beside him. They've pulled me away and I only stare and wait to wake from this nightmare.

His body is there.

And I'm holding to a lost moment.

Because I was right. The moment I stopped being angry, the moment the silence filled my ears like water, was the moment I wanted to die, too.

I want to die.

God, please. Please take me with him.

Stop punishing me.

ZOE

"ZOE BENSON? YOU ARE UNDER ARREST. YOU HAVE the right to remain silent . . ."

I don't feel them put the handcuffs on me. Only later, when they are taking them off at the police station, do I realize they had ever been there at all.

ZOE

THEY PUT ME IN A HOME. TWO HUNDRED MILES FROM my dad, who hasn't come to see me. They say he will come eventually, but I don't believe them, and I don't want him to.

I am lonely here.

I expect to be lonely forever.

They said they have it on tape, the homicide. They never call it murder and I won't, either. It was an accident. I tell myself that and they tell me, too. An accident. But I shouldn't have been stealing and I really shouldn't have run away. I should have stayed. Checked on the man. Waited for the police, they say.

I'm here because I didn't stay.

Will discharged one bullet from that gun. One bullet as he shoved me to the ground. No one knows where it went. Not at the cops, not at me. Out into space, maybe. I think it was just another accident. A jolt of his hands when he pushed me away.

That means he agreed with me, that we needed to give ourselves up and convince them it was all a misunderstanding. He didn't mean to die. It was an accident.

But they only needed one bullet from his gun to answer with ten of their own.

I miss him. I wish we'd done everything two people can do together when we had the chance. I wish I hadn't been afraid. Because that's all it ever was, fear.

I will never be afraid again.

I get another hearing in a few weeks. They have to figure out what to do with me then. In the meantime, I write bad poetry and draw Will as I remember him, not as he looked when the news covered the whole thing, the accident with the wine bottle, the murder in the desert.

There was no one there to watch Will's pine box get lowered into the ground. They didn't send him back to North Dakota but kept him in Nevada. It feels like he's not gone because I didn't see them put him under the sand.

The other girls here have done terrible things. I can tell because their eyes are hard and they look at me like the girls in Will's old home looked at me. Like I don't belong.

I tell myself I won't be lonely someday. I need to make myself believe I won't always be lonely, even though Will won't ever touch me again.

I'm empty here.

I need to get out so I can fill up and be whole again.

Will's car went to impound, but they cleaned it out and gave me everything inside. At least, that's what they say. There's so much missing. My chimes. His sweatshirt.

And *I'm* the thief, they say.

But I have the rest of his clothes, and I wear them even though they are too big. I sleep with his pillow and his blanket. I hold everything left of him to me as though it can soak through my skin and into my blood.

ZOE

I GET CHECKED ON A LOT. JUST PAIRS OF EYES popping in on occasion to look at me and a voice asking if I need anything.

What I really need is long gone.

The counselor here wants to talk about my dad, my mom. Will. The first thing I said to her was "No Will," as though thin wisps of him will leave me forever if I talk about him, memories escaping like smoke through a cracked window.

So she asks me about my mom.

I used to have nightmares. I saw my mom fall at all angles. Downstairs, upstairs, under the stairs. More and more I was the one at the top of the stairs, watching her tumble down.

I started pushing her in my nightmares. I wasn't just watching any longer; I put my hand out and shoved her down. In the morning I tried to remember that I wasn't the one who pushed her down, but the dreams slipped sloppily into reality like oil into water.

It was an accident, I tell the counselor, but still my fault, so I had to be punished for it.

She leans forward and eyes me carefully when I stop talking. Then I tell her the truth.

"I wasn't being punished because it was my fault my mom died. I was being punished because I had known the truth all along and never told anyone."

The counselor sinks back into her chair with a sigh and scribbles notes into my file.

She tells me about people who knew me, who saw things in another life, coming forward to tell stories.

That's why I'm here, really. Not because I ran. Not because I didn't tell. But because these people with stories to tell think they can help me now. They don't realize they already destroyed me with their silence all those years.

I hope all this sticks in their memories. A dead boy. Gunned down. An accident.

I hope that sticks like a dead mom, like a battered-child face never could.

If they let me leave the state one day, I'm going to get

to Vegas. I'm going to go to school and become something great, something useful, something that saves. I'm going to bring wrinkled babies into the world for moms and dads who want their children and I'm going to take home the ones who aren't wanted. I will put them in Little League and I will love them. I will do everything Will wanted me to do and more.

I am strong enough.

I know I am.

As soon as they let me out.

ACKNOWLEDGMENTS

A NUMBER OF WONDERFUL AND TALENTED PEOPLE
came together to help make me the writer I am and this
book the novel that it is. My heart swells with gratitude.

My large and supportive family—parents, stepparents,
brothers, sister, in-laws, aunts and uncles—have been
instrumental in shaping and championing my dreams and
goals, my expectations, and my successes. Thank you for
putting up with and loving unconditionally a girl who was
quirky and headstrong, and a woman who is even worse.

Infinite thanks, love, and moose-themed gifts to a group

of ladies who make me laugh, cry with me, offer advice, critique my work with astonishing insight and intellect, and *every single day* make this journey more fun than I'd thought possible: Amanda Hannah, Amy Lukavics, Emilia Plater, Kaitlin Ward, Kate Hart, Kirsten Hubbard, Kristin Otts, Kody Keplinger, Lee Bross, Leila Austin, Phoebe North, Sarah Enni Herness, Steph Kuehn, Sumayyah Daud, and Veronica Roth. One paragraph of thanks isn't enough, but not to worry—thirty years from now the memoirs will reveal all.

This book reached its potential thanks to the discerning eye and thoughtful considerations of my editor, Sarah Dotts Barley, who is a lady epitomizing grace and class and an absolute joy to work with. I am grateful to you and the entire team at Harper Children's who came together to produce this book.

My sincerest thanks to my incredible agent, Suzie Townsend, who has tirelessly supported my writing and promoted my career. You are an advocate of the highest order and a lovely friend. I am indebted to Joanna Volpe for the pass-along.

Thank you to Professor Juan Guerra for invaluable words of wisdom when they were most needed.

My eternal love and gratitude to two beautiful pixies who brought magic into my life and who also taught me to be better, to become the person they deserve.

Paul. The love of my life. Thank you for never doubting. Not for a single moment. And thank you for finding my artistic temperament amusing rather than annoying. I love this life with you.